THE MOTOR GIRLS ON CEDAR LAKE

OR

THE HERMIT OF FERN ISLAND

I0616933

Margaret Penrose

1st WORLD LIBRARY
Literary Society

The Motor Girls On Cedar Lake

Margaret Penrose

© 1st World Library – Literary Society, 2005
PO Box 2211
Fairfield, IA 52556
www.1stworldlibrary.org
First Edition

LCCN: 2005906533

Softcover ISBN: 1-4218-1589-3
Hardcover ISBN: 1-4218-1489-7
eBook ISBN: 1-4218-1689-X

Purchase *"The Motor Girls On Cedar Lake"*
as a traditional bound book at:
www.1stWorldLibrary.org/purchase.asp?ISBN=1-4218-1589-3

1st World Library Literary Society is a nonprofit
organization dedicated to promoting literacy by:

- Creating a free internet library accessible from any
computer worldwide.
- Hosting writing competitions and offering book
publishing scholarships.

Readers interested in supporting literacy
through sponsorship, donations or
membership please contact:
literacy@1stworldlibrary.org
Check us out at: www.1stworldlibrary.ORG
and start downloading free ebooks today.

The Motor Girls On Cedar Lake
contributed by Tim, Ed & Rodney
in support of
1st World Library Literary Society

CONTENTS

CHAPTER I

PUSHING OFF

"Oh, Cora! Isn't this perfectly splendid!" exclaimed Bess Robinson.

"Delightful!" chimed in her twin sister, Belle.

"I'm glad you like it," said Cora Kimball, the camp hostess. "I felt that you would, but one can never be sure - especially of Belle. Jack said she would fall a prey to that clump of white birches over there, and would want to paint pictures on the bark. But I fancied she would take more surely to the pines; they are so strong - and, like the big boys - always to be depended on. But not a word about camp now. Something more important is on. My new motor boat has just arrived!"

"Has it really?" This as a duet.

"And truly," finished Cora with a smile. "Yes, it has, and there is not a boy on the premises to show me how to run it. Jack expected to be here, but he isn't. So now I'm going to try it alone. I never could wait until evening to start my new boat. And isn't it lovely that you have arrived in time to take the initial run? I remember you both took the first spin with me in my auto, the Whirlwind, and now here you are all ready for the trial performance of the motor boat. Now Belle, don't refuse. There is absolutely no danger."

"But the water," objected the timid Belle.

"We can all swim," put in her sister, "and you promised, Belle, not to be nervous this trip. Yes, Cora, I'm all ready. I saw the craft as we came up. Wasn't it the boat with the new light oak deck and mahogany gunwale? I am sure it was,"

"Yes, isn't she a beauty? I should have been satisfied with any sort of a good boat, but mother wanted something really reliable, and she and Jack did it all before I had a chance to interfere."

"I wonder what your mother will next bestow upon you?" asked Belle with a laugh. "She has such absolute confidence in you."

"Let us hope it will not be a man; we can't let Cora get married, whatever else she may do," put in Bess, as she shook the dust from her motor coat, and prepared to follow Cora, who was already leaving the camp. Belle, too, started, but one could see that she, though a motor girl, did not exactly fancy experimenting on the water. It was but a short distance to the lake's edge, for the camp had been chosen especially on account of the water advantage.

"There she is! See how she stands out in the clear sunshiny water! I tell you it is the very prettiest boat on Cedar Lake, and that is saying something," exclaimed Cora, the proud possessor of the new motor craft.

"Beautiful," reiterated the Robinson twins.

"But what do you know about running it?" queried Belle.

"Why, I have been studying marine motors in general, and have been shown about this one in particular," replied Cora. "The man who ran it up from the freight depot for me gave me a few 'pointers,' as he called them."

She stepped into the trim craft and affectionately patted the shining engine.

"'It is much simpler to run than a car, and besides, there isn't so much to get in your way on the water," Cora went on.

"My!" exclaimed Bess as she stepped in after her hostess. "This is really - scrumptious!"

"You take the seat in the stern, Belle, and Bess, you may sit here near me," said Cora, "as I suppose you will be interested in seeing how it works. Oh! There is the steamer from the train. Hurry! Perhaps there are folks aboard we know. Let us act at home, and pretend we have been running motor boats all our lives."

Cora took her place at the engine and before Bess or Belle had really gotten seated she was turning on the gasoline.

"You see this is the little pipe that feeds the 'gas' from the tank to the carburetor," she explained. "Now, I just throw in the switch: that makes the electrical connection: then I have to give this fly wheel - it's stiff - but I have to swing it around so! There!" and the wheel "flew" around twice slowly and then began to revolve very rapidly. "Now we are ready," and the engine started its regular chug chug.

"How do you steer?" asked Bess anxiously, for the big steamer with its cargo of summer folks seemed rather near.

"I can steer here," and Cora turned a wheel amidships, "or one may steer at the bow. Suppose you take the forward wheel Bess, as I may, have enough to do to look after the engine."

"Very well," acquiesced the girl, "but I hope I make no mistakes."

"Oh you won't. Just turn the wheel the way you want to go. Now we'll hurry. I want to show off my boat."

Bess took up her place at the steering wheel and turned it so that the boat started on a clear course. Everything seemed to work beautifully, and presently Bess was so interested in the gentle swerving of the craft, as the rudder responded to her slightest touch, that she, too, thought it very much simpler than motoring on land.

"There are the Blakes!" suddenly exclaimed Belle. "See, they are waving to us."

"Yes," answered Cora as she snatched off her cap and fluttered a response to the folks on the steamer. "Bess, keep clear out. The landing is just over there! The steamer makes quite a swell."

Bess turned, but she did it too suddenly. A wave from the steamer caught them broadside, and drenched the girls before they knew what had happened.

"Oh!" screamed Belle, "- we are running right into the steamer!"

"Bess! Bess!" called Cora. "Turn! I can't connect -"

Shouts from the steamer added to their confusion. Would they be run down on this, their very first attempt at navigation?

"They are the motor girls!" Cora heard some one on the steamer shout, and while this much has been told it may be well to acquaint the reader with further details of the situation. The Motor Girls were friends whom we have met in the four previous volumes of this series entitled respectively: "The Motor Girls," "The Motor Girls on a Tour," "The Motor Girls at Lookout Beach," and "The Motor Girls Through New England." In each of these volumes we have met Cora Kimball, the handsome, dashing girl who conquers everything within reason, but who, herself, is occasionally conquered, both in the field of sports and in the field of human endeavors. It was she who had the first automobile, her Whirlwind and while out in it she had some very trying experiences.

In the first volume she managed to unravel the mystery of the road. Bess and Bell, the Robinson twins, were with her, as they were again in the second volume, the story of a strange promise. This promise, odd as it was, all three girls kept, to the delight and happiness of little Wren, the crippled child. Next the girls went to Lookout Beach, where they had plenty of good fun, as well as time enough to find the runaways, two very interesting young girls, who had decamped from the "Strawberry patch." It was like a game of hide and seek, but in the end the motor girls did capture the runaways. Then in the story "Through New England," it was Cora who was hidden away by the gypsies, and what she endured, and how she escaped were assuredly wonderful. There were brothers and friends of course, Jack Kimball being the most important person of the first variety, while Walter Pennington and Ed Foster were friends in need and friends indeed.

And now we find these same girls undertaking a new role - that of running a motor boat, the gift of Mrs. Kimball to her daughter, for that mother, in her days of widowhood, had learned how safe it was to repose confidence in her two children, Cora and Jack.

The camp at Cedar Lake had been taken by Cora and her friends for a summer vacation on the water, and now, after a day's run from Chelton, the home town, in their auto, the Flyaway, the Robinson girls had again joined Cora who had come up the day previous, with a maid to get the camp to rights.

The steamer was indeed too close! Cora was frantically trying to turn the auxiliary steering wheel, but Bess in her fright was turning the more powerful bow wheel in the very direction of danger!

"Oh! Mercy!" shrieked Belle. "We are lost!"

Another wave almost submerged them. The passengers on the steamer had all run to one side of their boat.

"Turn right!" shouted Cora as she jumped up and fairly jerked from Bess the forward wheel. "Turn to the right!"

CHAPTER II

THE HAUNTED ISLE

For some seconds no one seemed to know just what had happened. The steamer was clear, and the motor boat was running safely. Three very wet girls were thanking their good fortune that the water was their only damage - and water in the shape of a shower of spray is not much of a matter to complain of, after you escape a collision.

"What happened?" asked Belle, when she had the courage to uncover her eyes.

"Bess turned wrong," said Cora.

"I couldn't tell which way to go," put in the frightened girl. "I was simply stage-struck. But what saved us?"

"I jerked the wheel just enough to get a little to one side, and then the steamer had a chance to turn away," replied Cora. "I tell you we had a close shave, but that makes our first trip all the more interesting. Bess, can I trust you now to take my place while I look at that wheel? The rope may have slipped?"

"Oh, don't do anything," pleaded Belle. "Call to that boat over there, and let us have help. See, they are coming this way."

"Why, it's the boys - our boys!" exclaimed Cora. "Why have they gone out without telling me, when they knew I wanted to use my boat?"

In a canoe that looked like a big eel as it slipped over the water could be seen Jack, Ed and Walter.

"Well!" called Jack. "I like that! Where did you get the - ocean liner, Cora?"

"Don't say anything about the accident," she had a chance to whisper to the girls before replying to her brother. "I found my boat tied up at the dock," she answered gaily. "Isn't she a beauty?"

"What are you going to call her?" asked Walter.

"The Whirlpool, I guess," replied Cora, "that would go nicely with my Whirlwind, don't you think?"

"Oh, no, don't," objected Belle. "I should always feel that we were going to be -"

"Whirlpooled?" finished Jack. "Better make her the Petrel, Cora, for two reasons. We bought it from Mr. Peters, and she can walk on the water like the old original sea-fowl. Just see how she does saunter along."

"All right. Petrel will do, but it will be Pet for short," said Cora as now she allowed the boat to drift a little way from beside the boys' canoe.

"What was the matter with the steamer folks?" asked Ed. "Thought I heard something as we passed."

"Yes, you might have heard them talking about us if your ears had on their long distance," replied Cora quickly. "The Blakes are aboard."

"I saw their trunks at the station," said Jack "and they were tagged to The Burrow."

"That's the hole in the hill, isn't it?" asked Walter. "Well, I'm glad they have come up - the Benny Blakeses. I like a lot of folks around here. It is apt to have a depressing effect upon me if company is scarce and fishing shy."

"Or weather wet," put in Ed. "But say, Cora, I'd like to try the Pet." He remembered he was in a blue bathing suit, ever the most appropriate costume for a canoe. "But I'll wait until later, though I hate to. We have, as a matter of fact, an engagement at Far Island. Have you heard?"

"No, what?" asked the girls in chorus.

"Just a suspicion yet, but it may be true. We think - shall we give it away boys?"

"No; sell it," suggested Jack. "They sold us on this first trip, why should we give them anything?"

"Oh, Jack! You know I expected you to take me out the first time," said Cora reproachfully.

"Yes, and you know all about a boat, and start out without giving a fellow the slightest warning."

"But why didn't you come up when you knew the boat had arrived?" questioned the sister.

"Because - but that was what Ed was going to give away. It's a mysterious secret, and it is situated on Far Island. So long girls, I suppose you know how to land."

"Oh, yes indeed," said Cora in spite of the protest that was trembling on Belle's lips. "We started out, and we will get back all right. Wish you luck in whatever you are after," and she winked at Bess, who was now beside her at the engine, as Cora had concluded to guide the boat by the auxiliary steering wheel.

The boys veered off.

"I wonder what they are up to?" asked Cora. "As soon as we can do so, without being noticed, I think we will follow them. There must have been something important on, when Jack did not wait to take me out."

"Oh, don't let us go farther out on the lake," begged Belle. "I am nervous yet."

"Then suppose we take you in? Nettie is at the camp, and then Bess and I can go out to the island. There was really nothing the matter with the boat, the mistake was all due to our own nervousness."

"Well, I would feel better not to sail any farther," admitted the, pretty blond Belle, as she tossed back some of her breeze stray curls. "I am subject to sickness on the water, anyhow."

"On still water?" asked Bess archly. "Well, we will take you in, Twiny. And we will then go out. I want to redeem myself."

"Good for you, Bess," said Cora. "There is nothing like courage, unless it be gasoline," and after starting the engine, she turned the boat toward the shore. "There are the boys heading for the other island!" she exclaimed a moment later.

"They are trying to fool us. I wonder why?" asked Bess. "See, Belle. There are Nettie and Mary an shore - two of the best maids on the island. You will be all right with them, won't you, dear?"

"Of course," replied the twin, rather confusedly. "I don't need attention."

"But you are tired," put in Cora, "and those girls have not done a thing since lunch time. Just command them."

"'Very well. But do be careful, you two girls. A bad beginning you know."

"Oh, don't you worry about us," replied Cora confidently. "I feel as if this boat was a top in my hands. It is so much easier to handle than an auto. No gears, differentials or things like that. Good bye, Belle. Have supper ready when we return," and she sounded the small whistle that told of the start again.

"Good bye. Be careful," cautioned Belle. Then the two girls headed the craft for the little island around which they had just seen the boys disappear.

"I thought the boys looked very serious," said Bess, as she put her hand on the wheel Beside Cora's. "I wonder what is wrong?"

"Jack certainly had something very important on when he neglected me," said his sister. "I hope there is nothing really wrong. There are no people on that island, I believe."

"Then perhaps we had better not land?" suggested Bess. "It might be horribly lonely and we might not be able to find the boys."

"Well, when we get there we will be able to judge of all that," replied Cora. "Doesn't the Petrel motor beautifully?"

"And this lake," added Bess. "I never saw anything like it. Why some of those islands are big enough to inhabit."

"Yes, there is one island over there," answered Cora, pointing to the extreme eastern shore of the water, "and since I have seen it I am just dying to explore it. They call it Fern Island, and the store man tells the most wonderful tales about it. But we will have to wait until we all assemble. When did Hazel say she would come?"

"Tomorrow or next day. She has to take some special 'exams.' I am sorry that girl is so ambitious. It always interferes with her vacation."

"Hazel will make her mark some day, if she does not spoil it all by having someone make it for her - on a flat stone. But honestly Bess, I do hope she will come up before the others. Next to you and Belle I count more on Hazel Hastings than on anyone else in our party."

"And not a little on her brother Paul?" and Bess laughed in her teasing way. "Now Cora, Paul Hastings is acknowledged to be the most useful boy in all the Chelton set. He can fix an auto, fix an electric bell, fix an alarm clock -"

"And no doubt could overhaul a motor boat," finished Cora, as she turned the Petrel toward land. "Well, this is Far Island, and I am sure the boys headed this way. Let's shout."

Putting her hands to her mouth, funnel fashion, Cora sent out the shrill yodel known to all of the motor girls and motor boys. Bess took up the refrain; but there was no answer.

"If they were ashore wouldn't their boat be about?" asked Bess. "We can see all this side of the island, but you said it was too rocky to land on the other shore."

Cora looked about. Yes, one edge was all sandy and the other rocks. If the boys had come ashore they must have done so from the north side.

"My, what a lot of boats!" exclaimed Bess. "Cora, just see that flock," and she pointed to a distant flotilla of various craft across the lake.

"Yes, and so many canoes, we could hardly tell the boys in that throng. Do you suppose they are in that parade?"

"Oh, no. They had only bathing suits on, and that really looks like some fleet," replied Bess. "Yes, see there is their club banner. My! I had no idea that Cedar Lake boasted of such style."

"We may expect water picnics every day now," said Cora. "But just see that old man in the rowboat towing that pretty canoe. Do you suppose he has it for hire?"

"Likely. But how would anyone hire it out here? Why not from shore?" questioned Bess.

"Well, perhaps he is taking it to the dock," and Cora allowed her boat to touch the island shore. "At any rate if we are to find the boys we had better be at it, for I want to start back before that throng of boats gets in my way. I feel sure enough, but I like room."

Both girls stepped ashore as Cora caught the boat hook in the strong root of a tree and pulled the craft in. Then she shouted again.

"Jack! Jack!" she called. "Isn't it lonely here," she said suddenly, realizing that while she had expected the boys to be on the island, they might have gone to any of the other bits of land.

"Yes," said Bess. "I never felt so far away from everything before. On an island it is so different from being on real shore!"

"Yes, it is farther out," and Cora laughed at the description. "Bess, I guess I was mistaken. The boys do not seem to be here."

"Then do let's go back," pleaded Bess. "I am actually afraid."

"Of what? Not those 'jug-er-umms.' Just hear them. You would think the frogs were trying to drive us away from their territory."

"I always did hate the noise they make," declared Bess. "It sounds like a dead, dark night. Why do they croak in the daytime?"

"Night is coming," Cora explained, "and besides, it is so quiet here they do not have to wait for nightfall. But listen! Didn't you hear those dry leaves rustle?"

"Oh Cora, come!" and Bess pulled at her friend's skirt. "It may be a great - snake."

Cora stood and listened. "No," she said, "that was no snake. It sounded like something running."

"Come on, Cora dear," begged Bess, so that Cora was obliged to agree. "See, all the boats have gone the other way. And if anything happened we might just as well be on this desert island as on that desert water."

They had not ventured far into the wood, so that it was but a few steps back to the boat. Cora loosened the bow line and presently the engine was chugging away.

"Oh," sighed Bess, "I felt as if something dreadful was going to happen. Ever since those gypsies took you, Cora, I am actually afraid of everything in the country. It did seem safe on the water, but in those woods -"

"Now, Bess dear, you are to forget all about the gypsies. I have almost done so - that is, I have forgotten all the unpleasant part. Of course, I occasionally hear from Helka. Do you want to steer, Bess?"

"I would rather not," confessed Bess, "for I am actually trembling. Where do you suppose the boys could have gone?"

"Haven't the least idea, and we have no more time to speculate. There! Didn't you hear a strange noise on the island? I declare, that store man must be right. Those islands

Margaret Penrose

are haunted!"

"Wasn't that a queer noise! Oh! I am so glad we are safe in our boat," and Bess breathed a sigh of relief. "I would have died if that noise happened while we were there."

"But I should like to know what it is, and I will never be satisfied until I find out," declared Cora. "That was neither bird nor beast - it was human."

But the motor boat, girls headed straight for shore - the sun seemed falling into the lake as they reached the camp to be welcomed by Belle. The story of the trip to the island and the disappearance of the boys was quickly told.

CHAPTER III

WHAT HAPPENED TO THE BOYS

"What can have happened to the boys?" murmured Belle. "I am afraid they are drowned."

"All of them?" and Cora could not repress a smile. "It would take a very large sized whale to gobble them all at once, and surely they could not all have been seized with swimming cramps at the same moment. No, Belle, I have no such fear. But I am going right out to investigate. I know Jack would never stay away if he could get here, especially when he knew this would be your first evening at the lake. Why, the boys were just wild to try my boat," and she threw her motor cape over her shoulders. "Come on girls, down to the steamer landing. There may have been some accident."

Belle and Bess were ready instantly. Indeed the twins seemed more alarmed than did Cora, but then they were not used to brothers, and did not realize how many things may happen and may not happen, to detain young men on a summer day or even a summer night.

"Oh dear!" sighed Belle, "I have always dreaded the water. I did promise mamma and Bess to conquer my nervousness and not make folks miserable, but now just see how things happen to upset me," and she was almost in tears.

"Nothing has happened yet, Belle dear," said Cora kindly,

"and we hope nothing will happen. You see your great mistake comes from what Jack calls the 'sympathy bug.' You worry about people before you know they are in trouble. I feel certain the boys will be found safe and sound, but at the same time I would not be so foolhardy as to trust to dumb luck."

"You are a philosopher, Cora," answered the nervous girl, her tone showing that she meant to compliment her chum.

"No, merely logical," corrected Cora, as they walked along. "You know what marks I always get in logic."

"But it all comes from health," put in Bess. "Mother says Belle would be just as sensible as I am if she were as strong."

"Sensible as you are?" and Cora laughed. Bess had such a candid way of acknowledging her own good points. "Why, we have never noticed it, Bess."

"Oh, you know what I mean. I simply mean that I do not fuss," and Bess let her cheeks glow at least two shades deeper.

"Well it is sensible not to fuss, Bess, so we will grant your point," finished Cora as they stepped on the boardwalk that led to the boat landing. "Why, I didn't suppose they would light up with that moon," she said. "That's the old watchman over there."

A man was swinging a lantern from the landing. He held it above his head, then lowered it, and it was plain he was showing the light to signal someone on the water.

Cora's heart did give a quickened response to her nerves as she saw that something must be wrong. But she said not a word to her companions.

"What are they after?" asked Belle timidly.

"Probably some fishermen casting their nets for bait," Cora

answered evasively. "You stay here, while I speak with old Ben."

Bess and Belle complied, although Bess felt she should have been the one to ask questions. What if anything had really happened to the boys! Jack was Cora's brother.

"Have you seen anything of some boys in a canoe?" Cora asked of the man with the lantern. "They set out this afternoon, and have not yet returned."

"Boys in a canoe?" repeated Ben, in that tantalizing way country folk have of delaying their answers.

"Yes, my brother and two of his friends went out toward Far Island -"

"Fern Island?" interrupted the man.

"No, when we last saw them they were going away from Fern and toward Far Island," said Cora.

"Well, if they're on Fern Island at night I pity them. There ain't never been anyone who put up there after dark who wasn't ready to die of fright, 'ceptin' Jim Peters. And the old boy hisself couldn't scare Jim. Guess he's too chununy with him," and the waterman chuckled at his joke.

"But you have not heard of any accident?" pressed Cora.

"I saw them young fellers myself. They was in a green canoe; wasn't they?"

"Yes," answered Cora eagerly.

"Well, I asked Jim Peters if he had sawed 'em, and he said - but then you can't never believe Jim."

"What did he say?" excitedly demanded Cora, as Bess and

Belle stepped up to where she was talking.

"He said they had tied their boat up at the far dock, and had gone on the shore train to the merry-go-'round."

"But they were in their bathing suits!" exclaimed Cora.

"There! Didn't I tell you not to take any stock in Jim's news! I knowed he was fibbin'. But - say miss. There's this about Jim. He don't ever take the trouble to make up a yam unless he has a motive. Now I'll bet Jim knows something about them lads."

"Where does this man live?" asked Cora.

"He don't live no place in particular, but in general he stays at the shanty, when he ain't on the water. But he's a regular fish. The young 'uns calls him a fish hawk."

"How could we get to his place? Do you think he is at the shanty now?" went on Cora, determined to find out something of the man, for she had reason to believe that the dock-hand knew what he was talking about.

"Bless you, child! It ain't no place for young girls like you to go to any time, much less at night. But I'll tell you what I'll do. I'll jest take a look around myself. I sort of like a girl who knows how to talk to old Ben without being sassy."

"Thank you very much, Ben, but I really must hurry to trace the boys. I suppose you have no police around the island?"

"Wall, there's Constable Hannon. He is all right to trace a thing when you tell him where it is, but Tom Hannon hates to think." Ben raised the lantern above his head and then, as if satisfied that the signaling was all finished, he placed the lantern on a hook that hung over the edge of the dock.

"Oh, Cora," put in Bess, "it is almost eight O'clock. We must hurry along."

"I know, Bess dear, but I had to find out all this man knew. Now I am satisfied to start for the other end of the lake."

Cora's voice betrayed the emotion she was feeling in spite of her outward calm. The matter was now assuming a very serious aspect.

"One thing seems certain," she said to all who were listening, "they could not all have been drowned. They were all expert swimmers. Nor would they go to any merry-go-'round and leave us waiting for them. The question now is, what could have detained them?"

"Well, here comes Jim now," said Ben. "Just you keep quiet, and I'll pump him."

A man came slouching along the dock. He had the way of seeming much younger than he pretended to be - that is he walked with his head down although his shoulders were straight and broad as those of any well trained athlete. The three girls instantly decided that this man had some strange motive in his manner. He was shamming, they thought.

"Hello there, Ben," he called to the dock hand jokingly. "How's the tide?"

"Not much tide on this here lake," replied Ben sharply. "Never knowed much about them tides, as I've lived at this hole most all my born days. But how was business to-day? That was quite a fleet. How'd you make out?"

"Oh, same as usual," and Jim Peters looked from under his big hat at the girls. "Got company?"

"Yes, a couple friends of the old lady's. They're camping here."

"Oh," half-growled the man understandingly as he made his way to the water's edge.

"Where're you goin' now?" asked Ben.

"Up the lake," replied the man.

"Oh, say," spoke Ben as if the thought had just occurred to him, "where did you say them young fellers went? The ones who started out in a canoe?"

Now Cora saw that this was the man who had come down the lake with the canoe trailing behind his rowboat. He stepped into the lantern's light, and both Bess and Belle must also have recognized him, for they shot a meaning glance at Cora.

"What fellows?" drawled the man in answer to Ben's question.

"The ones I asked you about. You said they went to the merry-go-'round. Did they?"

"Yep," replied the man sententiously.

"Where is that?" asked Cora, unable to restrain herself longer.

"At the Peak," he said vaguely. Then he stepped into his rowboat and before anyone could question him further he was pulling up the lake.

"Well, I'll be hung! Excuse me ladies, but I am that surprised," said Ben apologetically. "Say, that fellow knows about the kids, and we've got to follow him. But how?"

"In my motor boat," proposed Cora quickly. "We could overtake him in that before he had any idea we were following him!"

"Have you a motor boat? Good! Where is it? Here, I'll call Dan. He kin run faster than a deer. Dan! Dan! Dan!" shouted the old man, and from a nearby rowboat, where, evidently, some boys were having some sort of a harmless game, Dan appeared. He was a tall youth, the sort that seems to grow near the water. "Hey Dan, I want you to go where this girl tells you, and fetch her boat," said Ben. "Quick now, we've got something to do."

"It's up at the new camp," said Cora. "It's the new boat you must have seen come up this afternoon."

"Oh, yes'm, I know it, and I know where it is," replied the lad, and then he was off, his bare feet making no sound. He called back through the darkness "Got any oil or gas?"

"Yes," replied Cora, and away he ran.

"Ain't he a regular dock rat," said Ben with something like pride in his voice.

"I hope we do not lose sight of that man," remarked Cora.

"Oh Jim can't pull as hard as he thinks, especially on a lazy day when he has been out some," affirmed Ben. "Now suppose you girls just sit on this plank while you wait? 'Twon't cost you nothin'."

He dusted off the big plank with his handkerchief, and upon the board, Cora, Bess and Belle seated themselves.

"I suppose Dan will haul the boat down," said Cora. "It isn't locked, but he may not want to start the motor."

"Oh, you can trust to Dan to get her here. When he isn't a dock rat he's a canal mule. There! Ain't that him? Yep, there he comes and he's got her all right," said old Ben proudly.

The boy could now be seen walking along the water's edge, as he pulled the motor boat by the bow rope. The girls were quick to follow Ben to the landing, and there all three, with Ben, got aboard.

The girls helped Cora light the port, starboard and aft-lights;

then they were ready to start.

"Better let me run her," said the man, "as I know all the spots in this here lake. Besides," and he touched the engine almost fondly, "there ain't nothin' I like better than a boat, unless it's a fish line."

"This is a very simple motor," explained Cora, showing how readily the gas could be turned on and how promptly the engine responded to the spark.

"It's a beauty," agreed Ben, as the "chugchug" answered the first turn of the flywheel.

Belle and Bess sat in the stem and Cora went forward. It was a delightful evening and, but for the urgency of their quest, the first night sail of the Petrel on Cedar Lake would have been a perfect success.

"Isn't that a light?" asked Belle, loud enough for Cora to hear.

"Yes. Ben see, there is a light. Do you suppose that is on Jim's boat?" asked Cora.

"Never," replied Ben, "he's too stingy to light up on a moonlight night when the water's clear. Of course the law says he must, but who's goin' to back up the law?"

"Which way are you going?" she questioned further.

"See that track of foam over yonder? That's Jim's course. We'll just pick his trail," said Ben. "Now there! Watch him turn! He's headin' for Far Island!"

At this Ben throttled down, and, a few minutes later he turned off the gas and cut out the switch.

"We'll just drift a little to give him a chance to settle," he said. "We don't want to get too close - it might spoil the game."

Belle and Bess were both too nervous to talk. It seemed like some pirate story, that they should be following a strange fisherman to a wild island in the night, in hopes of finding the boys - possibly captured boys!

Cora listened eagerly. She, too, was losing courage - it was so slight a hope that this man would lead them to where the boys might be.

"There! See that!" exclaimed Ben. "He's talking to some one on land."

"Yes, I heard Jack's voice," exclaimed Cora. "Oh, I am so glad they are safe!"

"But how do we know?" asked Belle, her voice trembling.

"Jack's voice told me," replied Cora, "for if they were in distress he would not have shouted like that!"

"But he was mad," said Ben, and in this the old fisherman made no mistake, for the voices of the boys, in angry protest, could be heard, as they argued with some one, who succeeded in keeping his part of the conversation silent from the anxious listeners.

CHAPTER IV

GETTING BACK

A few minutes later the rowboat of Jim Peters came out from Far Island, and in it were the boys!

"If we have to bale her out all the way" Ed was saying, "I can't see why we should pay you a quarter a piece. Seems to me we are earning our fare."

They were now almost alongside the drifting motor boat.

"Jack! Jack," called Cora. "We are here, waiting for you. What ever happened to you?"

"Well," exclaimed the boys in great surprise. "Glad to see you girls - never gladder to see anyone in my life. Can you take us on?"

"Of course we can," replied Cora. "My! We thought you were lost."

"Not us, but our boat," answered Walter. "Some one stole our canoe and left us on the island, high and dry."

"There," said Ben, "didn't I tell you?"

"Well, you fellows owe me just the same as if you went all the way," growled Jim Peters. "I've lost my night hire waitin' fer you."

"How'd you know about them, Jim?" asked Ben, in a joking sort of tone. "Wasn't it luck you happened up this way tonight?"

The other man did not reply. Cora had stepped down to the seat in front of the engine where Ben sat.

"Do you think that man stole their canoe?" she asked.

"Hush! 'Taint no use to fight with Jim. He'd get the best of you sure, and besides, then he would be your enemy. Just make a joke of it, and I'll tell you more later," and Ben prepared to start as soon as the boys, who were climbing into the motor boat, were ready.

"I'll pay you when we get to land," said Jack to the boatman, "I have no money in my bathing suit."

"Well, see that you do," said the man in a rough voice. "I'm not goin' to leave my work to tow a couple of sports just for the fun of it."

"Oh you'll get paid all right," Jack assured him, "and so will the fellow who stole our boat - when we catch him."

"I'll chip in for that," said Walter. "Never saw such a trick. Hello Bess, also howdy Belle. My, isn't it fine to be rescued from a desert island by three pretty girls?"

"Wallie! Wallie. There's a stranger aboard," warned Cora.

"Oh yes, this is Ben - Ben -"

"Just Ben," interrupted the man at the wheel, with a chuckle.

"But he has been so kind," added Cora. "Only for him we should never have found out where you were."

"If you hadn't taken us off that old sieve," put in Ed, "I think we would soon have had to swim back to the island. We never could have made the shore in that thing, neither could we swim that distance."

"S'long Jim!" called Ben, as the old rowboat was sent off in the darkness.

"See, he isn't balin' her now," he told the boys.

"How's that?" all asked in chorus.

"Oh, that's a great boat - leaks to order," replied Ben, as he turned over the fly wheel and Cora's craft shot swiftly away from the island.

The boys were too busy talking to the girls, and the latter were too busy asking questions, to go further into the matter of the leaking boat, but Cora did not fail to notice that the craft must have "leaked to order." "What could that man have intended doing? Did he want to sink the boat?" she was wondering.

"Well, if we haven't had a pretty time of it," said Ed. "First, we had to go up trees to get out of the way of something - we are not yet sure whether it was man or beast. Then when we crawled down, and made for the shore the canoe was gone clear out of sight."

"Haven't you any idea who took it?" Cora asked.

"Wish we had - I'll wager he would have to sleep out of doors to-night," threatened Jack. "It was the meanest trick."

Cora gave Bess the signal to keep still about having seen a canoe at the back of Jim Peter's rowboat that afternoon. Cora was convinced that Ben knew what he was talking about when he warned her to be careful of Jim Peters.

"But why did you go back to the island?" asked Cora. "I

thought you were going to spend the afternoon with us girls?"

"We were, then again we couldn't," answered her brother. "We had a very important appointment at Far Island."

"Ben, don't you want one of us to run her?" asked Ed. "We were to have had a try -"

"Nope. This here is the best fun I can have, and this boat is a beauty," replied the old man. "If I had one that could go like this and carry so many passengers I'd give up the dock."

"Yes, a boat like this would earn its own living," agreed Jack. "Run her as long as you like to, Ben. It gives us a chance - ahem -"

"To sit nearer your sisters," finished Ben, with a sly laugh.

"All's well that ends well," quoted Belle to Ed, for she was scarcely able yet to draw a free breath - her anxiety had been too keen. "I cannot believe that we are all here together again."

"Just pinch me," said Ed laughing, "and if I don't give our war whoop you may be sure this is not me - I am still on the Robinson ranch - there, that was an unpremeditated pun; I mean the old Robinson Crusoe and I forgot that he was great-grandfather to the present Robinson twins."

"Say, Ed," put in Walter, "what do you say if we buy a houseboat? This has the camp beaten to a frazzle."

"It's all right on such a night," replied Ed, "but houseboats, I believe, cost money, and our camp is rented to us for the season. Oh fickle Wallie! To fall in love with a motor boat, just because her name is Pet."

Walter was talking to Cora before Ed had finished speaking to him. That was Walter's irresistible way with the girls.

"No use talking, sis," said Jack, "this sail was worth being stranded for. If you are in no hurry, Ben, suppose we prolong it. Take us some place where we haven't been. You know the rounds of Cedar Lake."

This plan was agreed to, and, though the boys were not dressed as they would wish to have been, it was evening on the water, and their jersey suits were not altogether out of place.

"But what I would like to get at," began Ed, not being able to dismiss the subject, "is who stole our boat?"

"It may have drifted away," suggested Cora wisely. "There was a great fleet on the lake to-day, and any small boy might have let your boat go."

"Well, if I should lay hold of such a chap," declared Jack grimly, "he will grow up quickly. He will never be a small boy again."

"Now I'll tell you," offered Ben obligingly. "There's a lot of strange things likely to happen to you young 'uns while you're at this here lake. So take my advice an' go slow. Every one here goes slow, and it's the best way. If you suspicion a feller don't go at him. Just wait and he will walk right into your hands," and Ben sounded a warning whistle as he turned a point.

"He'll eat out of my hands if I get training him," prophesied Jack. "But all the same, Ben, I think that's first-rate advice. It saves us much trouble and that's the most important consideration. It takes time even to polish off such a specimen."

"And when you're done, you've got dirty hands," went on Ben in rough philosophy. "All the same, there is them that can't be otherwise dealt with, and when the time's ripe I'd - help myself. I know a man or two I'd like first-rate to get at, and stay at till I'd finished."

"Then, Ben," spoke Cora, "when you get your man we'll all help you, and when we get ours you can return the compliment."

Cora had a way of joking that invariably turned out prophetic - and this case was no exception.

"Well, if there ain't Dan sailin' around!" ex, claimed Ben suddenly. "He's lookin' fer me. Hey there, Dan! What's up?" he cried as he faced the boat with the brilliant lamp at the stern.

"Everything!" yelled back Dan. "Come up to the dock! There's trouble!"

Ben swung around the timer to gain more speed in a spurt of the motor.

"It's that Jim Peters, I'll bet," he declared, as they headed for Center Landing. "He's there ahead of us. He cut through the shallow channel."

Whether Jim Peters had taken leave of his senses or was simply unreasonably angry, folks were never able to say with certainty. At any rate, now, on this evening, the man seemed furious about something. No sooner had the motor boat come up to the dock to allow Ben to land, than Peters turned upon the young fellows he had been arguing with at the island, and in unmeasured terms spoke against all gasoline water craft. He said he couldn't see why the law allowed them to use the lake, for they made such a racket, filled the air with vile odors, and scared all the fish.

"You all ought to be arrested and deported!" he stormed. "The idea of peaceful folks being bothered with such nuisances! I'm not going to stand it if there's a law in the land! Why the idea! It's not right! I'll -" He stopped for breath.

"Now look here, Jim, you just quit!" said Ben quietly, as the fellow started off on another tirade, using still stronger language, and almost boiling over with rage. "Go easy," advised Ben. "There's that friend of yours, Tony Jones, comin'. Take a jab at him for a change."

As Ben got out, Jones sauntered along, and it was easy to see that, personally, he was quite a contrast to Jim. The situation seemed somewhat relieved.

"It's all right now," spoke Cora in a low voice, and with an easier air. "Let's go." With pleasant words for Ben and Dan she and her friends prepared to start off again. Walter gave the flywheel a few vigorous turns, but there was only a sort of apologetic sigh from the motor.

"Prime it a bit," suggested Ed.

With gasoline from a small oil can, Walter injected some of the fluid into the cylinder through the pet cock.

"Now for it!" he exclaimed. "Cross your fingers everybody," and once more he did the street-piano act, as Ed termed it. The engine only sighed gently.

Walter gave a quick glance over his shoulder toward the bow.

"Is that forward switch in?" he asked a bit sharply.

"Oh!" exclaimed Cora, "I accidentally pulled it out when I removed the bulkhead to look at the battery connections. There," she added after a quick motion, "it's in, Walter."

"Now for it! Hold your breaths," ordered the engineer. There was a sudden motion to the wheel, a whizzing buzz, a churning of the water under the stern and the boat moved away.

"We'll have to have a regular schedule - gasoline, switch, ground-wire, pet-cocks primed - oil cups up, and all that sort of thing," murmured Cora as they glided swiftly onward. "I'll print it on a card and hang it near the engine."

"Thanks," whispered Walter, as he took the wheel. "Where to?" he asked.

"The bath house," suggested Ed. "Our togs are there."

Gracefully the craft approached the group of bath houses, whence the boys had started in their canoe that afternoon. But no lights gleamed out to welcome the returning ones.

"My word!" exclaimed Walter a bit dubiously, "our togs are likely locked up in the safe, and here we are, forty miles from the pile of ready-to wear habiliments that hide behind Jack's trunk! Eh, what?"

"Sure thing!" agreed Ed with a sigh.

"Oh, never mind," consoled Cora. "Come over with us for a while, anyhow, if only to report progress."

CHAPTER V

A MAN IN THE SHADOW

When the engine had been carefully covered, on arrival at the camp dock, and the boat securely tied up for the night, the party were all literally shaking hands in gratitude for the rescue. It was only a short distance along the shore path to where the lads "bunked," but the young men shivered during the trip. The girls thought of their own coats and promptly offered them, for Walter, Ed and Jack were really suffering in their bathing suits.

"But we have heavy dresses on," insisted Cora, "and really Jack it is cool. Please take our coats," for her brother had objected.

"Well, if you insist," replied Jack, "but it seems to me we have had more than our share of bad luck for one day. First our boat is stolen, then our clothes are locked up. Who would think that that old boathouse man would go to bed so early."

"I am sure you are perfectly welcome to our coats," insisted Belle, as she and her sister divested themselves of their long automobile garments, "and they will look -"

"Lovely on us," put in Walter. "Let me have the blue one, please. It is so becoming."

Jack took Cora's heavy linen, Ed accepted the brown that Bess had worn, while Walter got the blue.

"Not so bad," said Jack, thrusting his hands deep into the patch pockets. "Don't know but what I'll get one like this, Cora."

"And I rather like the empire effect," said Ed turning around so that all, might admire the short-waisted coat he wore. "This is the Roman empire I believe, Bess; is it not?"

"No, the first Empire," corrected the girl. "My but you do look nice! You have a wonderful - outline."

"Yes, my nurse always complimented me on my outline. But do behold Wallie! Isn't he a peach?"

"He's a picture girl," declared Cora laughing. "Well, it is a good thing that we girls all wore coats when we went on the rescuing expedition. But say boys, what do you think was the trouble at the wharf? Ben seemed quite excited."

"I didn't like the looks of the fellow who offered us the boat ride," commented Ed. "And the queer part of it was, how did he know we were on the island?"

"And then his boat leaked and stopped. I'll bet his game was to make us fear drowning, and then save us at so much more per save. Like the philosopher and the ferryman, don't you know?"

"What philosopher?" asked Bess innocently.

"Oh, that old friend of mine who went to sea with his knowledge. Don't you remember?"

"I never heard of him," declared Bess falling into the trap.

"Then let me tell you," and Ed slipped his arm within hers as they walked along toward Cora's camp. "There was once a boatman and at the same time there was a philosopher. The former took the latter to sea, or to cross a small body of water, it doesn't really matter. All the way as they sailed the

42   Margaret Penrose

philosopher would say: 'Did you ever study astronomy?' The ferryman had not. 'Then half your life is gone,' said the philosopher. 'Did you ever study philosophy? No? Then another quarter of your life is gone.' And so on he went, Belle dear," continued Ed, "until suddenly the boatman interrupted him with: 'Say, did you ever study swimming?' And the philosopher admitted that he had not. 'Then,' said the boatman, 'the whole of your life is gone for this boat is sinking!' So you see, Belle, our boatman might have given us that little fairy story and charged accordingly."

"Yes, indeed!" put in Jack. "I think it was the luckiest thing that you girls came along. And Ben! We must give Ben a banquet or something fit."

"Ben is a great friend of mine," declared Cora. "I feel we would all have gone astray but for him. We girls would never have known enough -"

Then she stopped. She had no idea of telling the boys that they had followed Jim Peters with the hope of finding the missing ones whither he would lead them. Bess and Belle also had taken pains not to betray their story to the boys, for, as Cora said, Jim Peters was not a man to quarrel with, and the stolen boat was not a matter to joke about.

"Here comes Nettie!" exclaimed Belle. "I wonder what's her hurry."

"You've got company, miss," the maid said as she came up to the party walking toward the camp. "Miss Hasting and her brother have been waiting all evening."

"Hazel and Paul!" exclaimed Cora, almost running to the bungalow. "Oh, isn't that splendid!"

"And us in these!" wailed Walter. "Do you think Hazel will like me in baby blue?"

The boys really did look funny in the girls' long coats, but it all added to the merry-making. Paul Hastings was waiting outside the bungalow. He stood where the porch light fell upon him, and the girls all secretly agreed that he had grown handsomer since they had last seen him. Hazel, too, looked very attractive in her plain blue dress, with its turn-over collar and Windsor tie.

"What a pleasant surprise! We were afraid you would not come for some days Hazel!" said Cora in greeting.

"Oh, Paul had to come up here. Of course he has taken a position."

"What did I tell you!" cried Jack, folding the cloak about him in dramatic style. "Paul Hastings for the enterprise. Cedar Lake is the field; eh, Paul?"

"Well, I had a fine offer," said Paul modestly. "And I have been wanting to get out this way. They say there are all sorts of things to do in this locality."

"Looking for work! What do you think of that! Why, Paul dear, we are looking for a camp cook. Wallie nearly poisoned us on pancakes today," said Ed, "and if you would accept -"

"Come in doors," interrupted Cora. "We have had rather a strenuous afternoon, and I am almost tired. How did you get up from the train? Or did you come by boat?" she asked the new arrivals.

"A fellow rowed us up -"

"Yes and charged us fifty cents each," interrupted Hazel. "Wasn't that outrageous!"

"Some one like Jim Peters, I'll bet," said Ed. "But as Cora advised, let's go in doors. We really haven't dined!"

"Oh! you poor boys," cried Belle. "We almost forgot that you were stranded. Let me help Nettie fix up something."

"Yes, do. Fix up a lot of something," urged Jack. "That's the way I feel about it. But do we dine in these?"

By this time Hazel and Paul saw the queer attire of the three young men. Then a part of the situation was explained. The bungalow was one of those roomy affairs, built with a clear idea of affording every summer comfort. Cora was to be the hostess, and with her was the trusted maid, Nettie. There the girls were to visit as they chose, while the boys had taken a camp for themselves near the fishing grounds of the big lake.

"Now, make that coffee strong, girls," called Jack as the odor of the beverage came from the kitchen. "We are almost, if not quite, frozen."

He cuddled up on a big couch and threatened to do damage to Cora's pretty cloak.

"There's someone on the porch," suddenly whispered Bess, for a step sounded, so soft and stealthy, that she imagined someone was trying to look in the window.

"Yes, I heard it," said Ed, getting up and going to the door. A man stood in the shadow, stepping out quickly at the sight of the youth.

"I came for my money," he muttered. "You fellers ain't got no right to try to do me that way."

"Who tried to do you?" answered Ed, in no pleasant tones. "See here, Peters! This is not our camp, and we don't carry money in our bathing suits as we told you before. If you can't wait until to-morrow for the seventy-five cents you know what you can do."

"Oh I'll give it to you, Ed," said Cora, fearful that the man might become abusive. "I have plenty of small change."

She went into her room and got her purse. It was a pretty little affair, too frail to have been brought to camp, and too good to have left in the locked-up Chelton house. As she went back to Ed she held out the purse. "Here," she said, "take it and help yourself. My coffee will boil over."

Ed and Peters were standing near the edge of the porch. As Ed put his hand out to take Cora's purse it fell over the rail.

"Well," he exclaimed, "that's too bad. I must get a match."

At this Ed stepped to the door to ask for a box, while Peters hurried down the steps to look for the missing trinket. When Ed came back with a light Peters was looking industriously for the purse, but declared he had not seen it.

"Now see here, Peters," cried Ed angrily. "You have picked up that purse, and I want you to hand it right over here," and Ed dropped the cloak from his shoulders. "If you don't I'll teach you a lesson."

"Oh, you will, eh?" sneered the man. "Well you'd better get at it, kid," and with that he struck Ed a tantalizing blow on the cheek.

Ed clutched the man by the arm. By this time the confusion had been heard within doors, and the other boys hurried out.

"What's up?" asked Jack, just as Ed, with all his strength, almost bent the older man over backward.

Jim Peters was fairly roaring now. He was strong, but this young giant was a surprise to him, and after the way of the cowardly class, as soon as he found out he would be bested he "quit," and begged off.

"Hand me back that purse," demanded Ed. "I know you've got

it as well as if I had seen you take it."

"What's that over there?" snarled Peters, pointing to something bright in the grass.

Ed picked it up. It was the purse, but it was empty. Ed's exclamation told them that.

"My ring," cried Cora. "I had my ring - oh no. I forgot - that was not the purse," and Cora went in doors, presently returning with some small coins. "Here, Ed," she said, her voice trembling. "Do pay that man, and let him go. I - I am so frightened!"

"Cora," whispered Bess, "was your ring in that purse?"

"Hush," cautioned the other girl. "Let us try to make things brighter. Since that man sailed down the lake to-day with our boys' canoe we have had nothing but mishaps. Now let him go. I'll manage to reckon with him without endangering the life of anyone. He's too desperate a character to deal with in the ordinary way. Remember what Ben told us."

CHAPTER VI

CORA EXPLOITING

There had been three delightful days at Camp Cozy. Cora managed most of the delight, with the able assistance of Belle and Bess, while Hazel did much toward discovering things that she declared all the girls ought to know, for Hazel's happiness was ever in obtaining knowledge.

The boys had almost lost hope of getting back their canoe. They had searched the lake from shore to shore, offered rewards and had gone through the rest of the lost formula, but the boat was not returned.

Cora kept to herself her suspicions about Jim Peters. She also said nothing of the ring that was in the purse when it left her hands, but not in it when the purse was returned to her.

It was a splendid morning for a trip on Cedar Lake, and although Belle and Hazel had planned a trip to the woods, Cora and Bess were going out in the Petrel.

Passing Center Landing, Cora called a pleasant good morning to Ben, who sat on the end string piece, his feet aiming at the water and his broad brimmed hat caught on halo fashion at the back of his neck.

"Oh, I must ask him something," said Cora, suddenly turning her boat toward the wharf. She drew near enough to speak quietly.

"Ben," she said, "where is that shanty you told me about - Jim Peter's place?"

"Lands sake miss! you ain't goin' there?" asked the man in some alarm.

"Why not?" demanded Cora. "Can't I take care of myself in broad daylight?"

"But you don't know how ugly that feller can be," insisted Ben. "I tell you miss, I'd give him plenty of room, if I war you."

"Don't go," urged Bess.

"But, Ben," argued Cora, "I am afraid you have all let Jim Peters bully you. I am going to try him another way. Where does he live?"

"Well a hour ago he went up the lake. He goes up there every mornin' regular. Like as if he had some important business on the island. When I asked him about it he said there was a fellow who had some dangerous disease, and was campin' out there, and Jim allowed that he had to fetch him things."

"Indeed!" exclaimed Cora. "That's a queer story for a man like Peters. But I'm going to his shack first, even if he is not at home. It would suit me just as well to find him out on my first visit."

"But that young feller who lives with him? He's just as sassy as Jim, when he's around the shack. Of course he don't stay there always, as Jim does."

"Who is he?" questioned Cora. "I hadn't heard of such a person."

"Oh, he gives the name of Jones but it don't fit him fer a cent. I wouldn't be surprised if his real name was Macaroni or even Noodles. He's foreign, sure."

Cora laughed. "And he's young, you say?"

"A lot younger than Jim, but he could be that and yet not be very young, fer I guess Jim has lost track of time," replied Ben. "Yes, Jones is a swell, all right."

"But the shack? Where is it? I must be off," insisted Cora.

"It's quite a trip down the lake. Then you come to a point. Go to the left of the point, and when you come to a place where the willows dip into the lake, get off there. The shack is straight back in the deepest clump of buttonball trees."

"All right Ben, and thank you," said Cora as she started up the motor. "I feel like exploring this morning, and your directions sound interesting. I will come back this way to show you that I am safe and sound," and with that she sheered off.

"I hope it will be all right," faltered Bess. "Cora, are you never afraid to risk such things?"

"What is there to risk? The land is public, and we have as much right to follow that track as has Jim Peters or Mr. Jones. I wonder what Mr. Jones is like?"

"Maybe he would be very nice - a complete surprise," ventured Bess, at which remark Cora laughed merrily.

"You little romancer! Do you imagine that anyone very nice would chum in with Jim Peters? Isn't there something in your book about birds of the same quills?"

"It's aigrettes, in my book," retorted Bess. "But it all applies to the same sort of birds. Just the same, I am interested in Mr. Jones."

"I fancy perhaps that we are," said Cora. "But there is the point Ben spoke of. We are to turn to the left."

Gracefully as a human thing, the boat curved around and made its path through the narrow part of the lake.

"And there are the willows," announced Bess, as she saw the great green giants dipped into the water's surface.

"Yes. I thought it would be much farther on. But this is an ideal spot for hiding. One could scarcely be found here without a megaphone."

"Hear our voices echo," remarked Bess. "An echo always makes me feel desolate."

"Don't you like to hear your own voice?" asked Cora lightly. "I rather fancy listening to mine. An echo was always a delight to me."

"There's a man sitting under that tree!" almost gasped Bess.

"So there is, and I am glad of it. He will be able to direct us. I shouldn't be surprised if he were Mr. Jones," said Cora turning the Petrel to shore.

Under a big willow, in a sort of natural basket seat, formed by the uncovered roots of the big trees, a man sat, and as the boat grazed the shore, he looked up from some papers he held in his hands. Cora could see that he was very dark, and had that almost uncomfortable manner of affecting extreme politeness peculiar to foreigners of certain classes, for, as she spoke to him, he arose, slid the paper into his pocket, and bowed most profusely.

"I am looking for the cabin of Mr. Peters," said Cora, stepping ashore toward the tree. "Can you direct me to it?"

"The cabin of Mr. Peters?" and when the man spoke the

foreign suspicion was confirmed. "Why, who might Mr. Peters be?"

"Jim Peters; don't you know him?" asked Cora determined not to be thrown off the track. "He lives just in here - I should think in that grove -"

"Oh, my dear miss no! You are mistaken. No one lives around here. I am simply a rustic, looking about. But Jim Peters?"

"Are you not Mr. Jones?" blurted out Cora.

In spite of himself the man started.

"Mr. Jones?" he repeated. "Well, that name will do as well as any other. But allow me to tie your boat. Then I will take pleasure in showing you one of the prettiest strips of land this side of Naples."

"Oh, thank you. I have secured it," said Cora. "But I would like to explore this island."

Bess tugged at Cora's elbow. "Don't go too far. I am afraid of that man," she said in a whisper.

"Were you drawing as we came up?" Cora asked the stranger. "This is an ideal spot for sketching."

"Yes, I was drawing," he replied.

"Couldn't we see your picture?" asked Cora. "I do so love an outline."

"Oh, indeed it is not worth looking at. I must show you something when I have what will be worth while. This is only a bare idea."

"Well," said Cora starting off through the wood, "I must look for a cabin, or something like it. I have particular business with

Jim Peters."

"But you will only hurt your feet miss," objected the man. "Allow me to show you the island," and he bowed again. "Such wild swamp flowers I have never seen. It is the everglades, and well worth the short journey."

There was something about his insistent civility that betokened a set purpose, and since Ben (what a wonder Ben was) had told Cora that a man named Jones "hung out" with Jim Peters, Cora instantly guessed that this was the man, and that he was determined to keep her away from the shack. The situation gave zest to her purpose. Bess was fairly quaking as Cora could see, but what danger could there be in insisting upon finding that shack?

"I have only a short time to be out," objected Cora, "and perhaps some other time I will come to see your everglade. Come, Bess, I see a path this way, and I fancy if we follow it we will find an end to the path," she concluded.

"But may I not have the pleasure of your name?" the man called after her. "Perhaps we might meet -"

"Don't," whispered Bess. "Pretend you did not hear him."

"Oh, just see those flag lilies!" Cora called to Bess, covering the man's question without answering it. "Let us get some."

"Oh, aren't they beautiful!" replied Bess, in a strained voice. "I certainly must secure some of those."

They hurried away from the dark-browed man. He took his hand out of his pocket and upon the smallest finger his eyes rested. He sneered as he looked at a diamond ring that glittered on that slim brown finger.

"Foolish maid," he said aloud, and then the web of a strange force threw its invisible yet unbreakable chains over the summer life of Cora Kimball.

CHAPTER VII

DEEP IN THE DARK WOOD

"Cora, dear, please do not go any farther. Somehow I am afraid that man will follow us."

"Why, Bess! I thought you were going to be interested in Mr. Jones," and Cora stooped to pick up a wonderful clump of flag lilies.

"Jones! How could he be a Jones? He's a Spaniard."

"I thought so myself, Bess. But we do not have to plant his family tree. Now don't be a baby, girlie," and Cora squeezed the plump hand that hung so close to her own. "Let us get to the shack, and see if the boys' boat is about there. I am determined to run down Jim Peters."

Bess sighed. When Cora was determined! But the man had left the water's edge.

"Cora, see!" said Bess. "He is getting into a boat!"

"Yes and the boat belongs to Peters. There! He is surely the one who helps Jim out in all his affairs. Now we may seek the shack in safety," said Cora, as she watched the man at the water's edge push off. "I know the shack is over there, for I smell smoke in that direction. But we will turn the other way until he has cleared off," finished Cora as she and Bess stepped lightly over the dainty ferns that nestled in the damp earth.

"He is quite a boatman," remarked Bess, watching the man ply his oars, and make rapid progress up the lake.

"Yes, he must have been brought up near the water," replied Cora. "They say such skill as that is not accomplished on dry land. Jack always declared he could tell a fellow at college who had ever been near the water when a lad. They take to it like a duck."

"You can easily see that he is a foreigner," went on Bess with her speculations. "He must either be an Italian or a Spaniard."

"Now we may turn up the path. Yes this is a path, for everything is trodden down on it," declared Cora. "I hope the hut will not be too deep in the wood."

"We won't go if it is," objected Bess. "I don't fancy being taken captive by any wild woods clan."

"There," exclaimed Cora. "I just caught sight - of - it's a woman's skirt!"

"Yes, and there is a woman in it," added Bess. "See, here she comes."

"No, I don't think she does. I think she is standing still. We must have frightened her."

"What a looking - woman!"

"Great proportions," described Cora. "I guess wherever she lives they must feed her well."

Cora led the way, and Bess timidly followed.

"Don't go too near," whispered the latter.

"Why, she cannot eat us," replied Cora, smiling over her shoulder to the timid one.

"Well, what do you want?" roared the woman, as soon as she could be heard by the young ladies.

"We are looking for Jim Peter's shack," replied Cora bravely. "I have been sent here to speak with him."

"Have, eh? Well go ahead. Speak with me. I'm Mrs. Jim Peters," said the woman with a sneer.

"My business is with him," again spoke Cora, not in the least frightened by the voice which she knew was made coarser just to scare her.

"Well, he don't have no business that ain't mine," said the woman, "'specially with young 'uns like you, so you kin just clear off here before I -"

"Come on Cora," begged Bess. "I am shaking from head to foot."

"All right, dear," replied Cora, in a voice for Bess alone. "But, Mrs. Peters, can you tell me when your husband will be about here? I have some work to do on a boat and I understand he does that sort of thing."

The woman's face changed. "If that's what you want I'll tell him. You see it is always best to let the woman know first, fer Jim does do some foolish things. But just now he's got one boat to do?"

"I wonder if he might have a canoe to sell?" interrupted Cora, as the thought of thus trapping the woman occurred to her.

"He will have one in a few days," the other 'answered. "But it has to be fixed up."

"Could I see it?" asked Cora. "I may not be able to get over here again."

"Well, the shack is locked and I couldn't show it to you, but when Jim comes I'll tell him. Who will I say?"

Cora hesitated. "I hardly think it will be worth while really to order it," she said, "as I must have my brother look it over. I have a motor boat."

"I heard it chuggin' and I thought that lazy Tony had got a new way of wastin' his time. Tony is all right at writin' letters but he's a lazy bones else ways."

"Who's Tony?" asked Cora as if indifferently.

"He's Jim's side partner. Say, girl, I'll just tell you. I came up here a few weeks ago from a newspaper advertisement. I never knowed Jim Peters before, but if them two fellers think I'm goin' to cook in that hut and never go no place off this dock they're foolin' themselves. They don't know all about Kate Simpson."

Both girls were utterly surprised by her change of manner. Cora was quick to take advantage of it.

"You are quite right," she said. "This is no place for a lone woman, and some day when I have my brother along I will fetch my boat, and show you the big islands about here. It would do you good to get out in the clear - away from these dense woods."

"That it would, and I'm obliged to you miss," said the woman while Bess fairly gasped. "I want to go to one island - Fern Island they call it. Have you ever been there?"

"I know where it is," replied Cora, wondering what the woman's interest in that place might be. "I have been all around it."

"They say it's haunted," and the woman laughed. "It's a great game to put a haunt on a place to keep others off."

"Well, some day when you can leave your work, I'll take you over there," and Cora meant it, for she had not the slightest fear, either of the woman or her rough ways.

Besides, she felt instinctively that the woman's help would be valuable in the possible recovery of her ring and of the lost canoe.

"I'll be goin' back to the shackt fer if Jim comes along held raise a row fer me talkin' to strangers. You'd think I was looney the way he watches me."

"And is he a stranger to you?"

"Well, to tell the truth my mother and Jim's was cousins, but I never knowed him to be such a poor character as he is, or I'd never have come up here. But I don't have to stay all summer,"' she finished significantly.

"Well, good-bye, and I'll see you soon again," said Cora turning toward her boat.

"Good-bye, miss, but say," and she half whispered, "is that girl dumb?"

Cora burst out laughing. Bess a mute!

"No indeed, but she always lets me do the talking," answered Cora with a sty look at the blushing Bess.

"She has good sense, fer you know how to do it," declared Kate Simpson.

They could hear her bend the brush as she passed up the narrow way.

"What a queer creature," remarked Bess, when she felt that it was safe to try her voice.

"She is queer, but I think she knows a lot about things of interest to us. What did you think of her remark about Fern Island? To that pretty little spot we will make our next voyage," declared Cora, pulling on her thick gloves and taking her place in front of the motor. "Turn out into the open lake," she told Bess as they started off. "We will make a quick run and get back to the bungalow before the others have done the marketing. I am glad it is not our turn to get the lunch for I want to make a trip to Fern Island directly after we have had a bite. Seems to me," and she increased the speed of the engine a little, "it takes more time to get a meal at camp than it does at home. The simple life certainly has its own peculiar complications."

"Oh, there comes that man back! I am so glad we are away from that place," exclaimed Bess, as the boat of Jim Peters, with the smiling foreigner called "Jones" floated by.

CHAPTER VIII

THE HAUNT OF FERN ISLAND

The four motor girls started out in the Petrel. Never had the lake seemed so beautiful, nor had the sky appeared a deeper, truer blue. The pretty Placid lake was dotted all over with summer craft, the sound of the motor boat being almost constant in its echoing, "cut-a-cuta" against the wonderful green hills that banked shore and, island.

Hazel was steering, and of course Cora was running the engine. The pennant waved gaily from the bow of the boat, and of the many colors afloat it seemed that those chosen by the motor girls shone out most brilliantly on the glistening, silvery waters.

"I'm not a bit afraid now," admitted Belle, "I do think it is all a matter of getting used to the water. I thought I should never breathe again after that first day we went out."

"Yes," said Cora, "the water has a peculiar fascination when one is accustomed to it, and I am sure Belle will want to live on a houseboat before we break camp. There go the boys! What a fine motor boat!"

"Yes," said Hazel, "that's one from Paul's garage. Paul promised Jack he would speak to Mr. Breslin, the owner, about letting it out for the summer, as the Breslin family is not coming out here until later. It's the Peter-Pan, and the fastest boat on the lake."

"See them go! I guess they don't see us,"' remarked Belle.

"I am glad they do not," Cora said, "for I want to do some exploring, and if the boys came along they would be sure to have other plans for us. Now, Hazel, run in there. That is Fern Island."

"Oh, there's a canoe!" exclaimed Belle. "See! and a girl is paddling. What a queer looking girl!"

"Isn't she!" agreed Bess. "Why she has on a man's hat!"

"She sees that we are watching her. Look how she is hurrying off," remarked Cora. "I wonder how far this cove goes in?"

"We had better not try to find out," cautioned Belle. "I think we have had enough of happenings around here. This is where the boy's boat was stolen from; isn't it?"

"No, it was over there, but I guess we will put in at the front of the island, as there is no telling how deep the cove is," said Cora. "But see that girl go! Why she's actually gone! Where can she have disappeared to?"

"This ought to be called the 'disappearing' land," suggested Hazel. "I was sure that little canoe was directly in front of us, but now it is out of sight."

"Maybe that is the 'Haunt Girl of Fern Island,'" ventured Cora with a laugh. "I got a pretty good look at her, and I am willing to say she looked neither like a summer girl nor a winter girl - that is, one who might live here the year around. But just what sort of girl she might be I shouldn't like to speculate. Her hair got loose as she hurried, and she reminded me of some wild water bird."

"Be careful getting out," Belle cautioned Bess. "This new boat is new to slipperiness."

"Oh, I will get hold of a tree branch," Bess replied. "Then, if the boat drifts out, I can swing to safety."

All were ashore but Bess, and as such things often happen when they are looked for, the Petrel did careen from the waves of a passing launch, and just as Bess grasped an overhead willow branch, the boat swung out and she sprang in. Everybody laughed, but Bess lost her breath, a condition she disliked because it always added to the deep color of her plump cheeks.

"There!" cried Belle. "Didn't I tell you?"

"I wish that next time, Twin, you would leave me to guess!" exclaimed the other twin, rather pettishly.

"Isn't this perfectly delightful!" exclaimed Hazel, running over the soft earth where ferns were matted, and wild flowers grew tangled in their efforts for freedom. "I never saw such dainty little flowers! Oh! they are sabatial I have seen them in Massachusetts," and she fell to gathering the small pink blooms that rival the wild rose in shade and perfume.

"Here are the Maiden Hair ferns," called Cora. "No wonder they call this Fern Island."

"Let us see how many varieties of fern we can gather," suggested Belle. "I have ferns pressed since last year, and they look so pretty on picture mats."

At this the girls became interested in the number of ferns gatherable. Belle went one way, Bess another, and so on, until each had to call to make another hear her.

Cora ran along fearlessly. She was diving very deep into the ferny woods, and she was intent on coming out first, if it were only in a race to get ferns.

Suddenly she stopped!

What was that sound?

Surely it was some one running, and it was none of the girls!

Standing erect, listening with her nerves as well as with her ears, Cora waited. That running or rustling through the leaves was very close by. Should she call the girls?

But before she could answer herself, she saw something dart across a big rock that was caressed by a great maple tree that grew over it.

"Oh!" she screamed involuntarily. Then she saw what it was. A man, a wild looking man, with long hair and a bushy beard.

He had stopped just long enough to look in the direction of Cora. She saw him distinctly. Oh! if he should run toward Bess or Belle! Hazel would not be so easily alarmed but surely this was a wild man if ever there was such a creature.

"That is the ghost of Fern Island," Cora concluded. "I must get back to the girls."

She turned and hurried in the direction from which she had heard voices. "If they have not seen him," she reflected, "I will not say anything until we get back to camp."

"I have ten different kinds of ferns," suddenly called Belle, in a voice which plainly said that no wild man had crossed her path.

"I've got eight," said Hazel. "How many have you, Cora?"

Cora glanced at her empty hands. She had dropped her ferns.

"I have tossed away mine. I was afraid of black spiders," she said evasively.

"Isn't that too bad," wailed Bess, "and none of us picked any maiden hair because we thought you had it. Let us go and get some."

"Oh, I think we had best not this time," said Cora quickly. "I really want to get to the post office landing before the mail goes out. We can come another time when I have something to kill spiders with. I never saw such huge black fellows as there are around here." This was no shading of the truth, for indeed the spiders around Cedar Lake did grow like 'turtles', Jack had declared.

"Oh, all right," agreed Belle. "But this is the most delightful island and I am coming out here again. I hope the boys will come along, for there are such great bushes of huckleberries over there that we simply couldn't climb to them alone."'

"We will invite them next time," said Cora, and when she turned over the fly wheel of her boat her hands that had held the ferns were still trembling. She looked uneasily at the shore as they darted off.

"What's the matter, Cora?" asked Hazel. "You look as if you had seen the ghost of Fern Island."

"I have," said Cora, but the girls thought she had only agreed with Hazel to avoid disagreeing.

"What boat is that?" asked Bess a moment later, looking at a small rowing craft just leaving the other side of the island.

"It's Jim Peters'" replied Cora, "we were lucky to get back into ours before he saw it. I wouldn't wonder but what he might like to take a motor boat ride in the Petrel."

"Do you suppose he really would steal a boat?" exclaimed Belle.

"He might like to try a motor, I said," replied Cora. "They say that Jim Peters tries everything on Cedar Lake, even to running a shooting gallery. But see! He is reading a letter! Where ever did he get a letter on this barren island?"

"Maybe he carries the mail for the ghost," said Hazel, with a laugh.

CHAPTER IX

JACK AND CORA

"Cora, where is your ring?"

The sister looked at her finger. "Oh Jack," she replied, "I will get it - but not just now. Why?"

"I thought you always wore that ring when you put on your frills, and I haven't seen you so dressed up since you came to camp. Somehow, Cora, I feared you might have lost it."

"I did," she said simply.

"Your new diamond!"

"Yes, but I feel sure of finding it. Now, Jackie dear, please don't cross question me. I shouldn't have taken it off, but I did, so and that is how I came to lose it. But I want to tell you something while we are alone. I saw the ghost of Fern Island to-day."

"Nonsense! A ghost?" sneered Jack. "Why, Cora, if the other girls said that I should laugh at them."

"Well I want to tell you. We were on the island-the girls and I - and I got a little away from them when suddenly the wildest looking man rushed across the path. He had a beard like Rip Van Winkle and looked a lot like him too."

"Rip might be summering out this way, though I rather thought he had taken a trip in an airship," said Jack. "But honestly, Cora, what was the man like? Paul had a story of that sort. He declares he, too, saw this famous ghost."

"Do you suppose he might have taken the canoe? The wild man I mean. We saw a strange looking girl in a canoe and somehow she vanished. We could see her boat and then we couldn't, although we could not make out where she went to. It was the queerest thing. There must be some strange curves on those islands."

"Oh there are, lots of them. They are as curvy as a ball-twirler's best pitch. But the ghost. That is what interests me, since - ahem - since he has a daughter. Was she pretty?"

"I should say she was rather pretty," replied Cora, quite seriously, "but she did have a wild look too. I do believe she is a daughter to the wild man, whoever he may be."

"Well, everyone around here declares that is land is haunted, but fisher-folk are always so superstitious. Yet we must hunt it up. I will go out with you the next time you go. Did the other girls see him?" went on the brother.

"No, and I decided not to tell them. You know how timid Bess and Belle are, and if they thought there was such a creature about the island I would never get them to put foot on shore there again, and I do so want to investigate that matter. I believe Jim Peters has something to do with it for I saw him coming away from there with a letter. Now what would he be doing with a letter out on a barren island?"

"Oh Jim is a foxy one. I wouldn't trust him as far as the end of my nose. But here come the others. Will you go over to the Casino this evening."

"Yes, we had planned to go. That is why I am dressed up. Hazel may have to go to town to-morrow, and I want her to see something before she goes," replied Cora, just as the girls, and Walter, Ed and Paul strode up to the bungalow.

"Oh! we have had the greatest time," blurted out Bess. "Cora, you should have been with us. Ben got angry with Jim Peters, and he and Dan threatened to throw Jim overboard, and -"

"Jim seems to have a hankering after fights," put in Ed. "I haven't settled with him yet."

"Ed, you promised me you would call that off," Cora reminded him. "You know it was all about me, and you have given me your promise not to take it up again. That Jim Peters is an ugly man."

"All the same we heard that you were not afraid of him," said Walter with a tug at Cora's elbow. "Didn't you beard the lion in his den?"

"Who said I did?" asked Cora flushing.

"I promised - crossed my heart not to tell," said Walter. "But all the same the folks at the landing are talking about the pretty girl who went all the way up the cove, and stopped at the place where Peters and his pal land. I would advise you to be careful. They say that tribe is not of the best social standing," went on Walter quite seriously.

"I won't go there again," put in Bess.

"What! Were you along?" demanded Jack. "Then you must have been the pretty girl referred to at the landing."

"I was a pretty scared girl," declared Bess. "I tell you, I don't want to meet any more Peters or Joneses or Kates," she finished.

"But what was the trouble between Jim and Ben?" asked Cora.

"Let me tell it," Belle exclaimed. "We were just standing by the boathouse, watching some men fish, when Jim Peters, came along. He stopped and took a paper out of his pocket. The wind suddenly blew up -"

"And took the paper out of his hand," interrupted Hazel. "It blew across to where Dan was standing, and what was more natural than that Dan should pick it up?"

"And did Jim get angry at that?" inquired Cora.

"Angry! He fairly fell upon poor Dan," put in Walter, "and when Ben saw him - I tell you Ben may stand a lot of trouble on his own account, but, when it comes to anyone trying to do Dan, Ben is right there to fight for him. Didn't he almost put Jim over the rail?"

"There must have been quite a lively time," said Jack. "Sorry I missed it. There is so little excitement around here that we need all we can get. And what was the answer?"

"Jim took his old letter and slunk off," finished Belle. "And Dan said he couldn't have read even the name on the out side if he had tried. He said it must have been written in Greek," and Belle laughed at the idea of the classics getting mixed up in any such small affair.

"Seems to me," said Cora thoughtfully, "that Jim had some very important reason for fearing that one might see that letter."

"Yes," declared Hazel, "that struck me right away. I shouldn't be surprised if it had been addressed to - the ghost!"

"Well, if you young ladies intend to see what is going on at the Casino this evening," Ed reminded them, "we had better make a start. This is amateur night, I believe."

"And the Blake girls are going to sing," announced Jack.

"Then I shall have a chance to clap my hands at pretty Mabel," and he went, through one of those inimitable boys' pranks, neither funny nor tragic, but just descriptive.

"I think it is awfully nice of the Blake girls to take part," said Cora, "for in this little summer colony everyone ought to be agreeable."

"But I notice you are not taking part," Ed said with a laugh. "Just fancy Cora Kimball on the Casino platform."

"Don't fancy anything of the kind," objected Bess. "We are willing to be sociable but we have no ambition to shine."

"Come along," called Jack, who was on ahead with Hazel, "and mind, if anything brushes up against you, it is apt to be a coon, not a cat, as Belle thought the other night."

They started off for the path that led to the public pavilion on the lake shore. Cora was with Ed, Walter had Belle on one side and Bess on the other, because he declared that the twins should always go together to "balance" him. Jack and Hazel led the way.

At the pavilion the seats were almost all occupied, for campers from all sides of the lake flocked there on the entertainment evenings. A band was dreaming over some tune, each musician evidently being his own leader.

The elder Miss Blake, Jeannette, who sat on an end seat, arose as they entered and made room for the Chelton folks to sit beside her, meanwhile gushing over the prospect of the evening's good time, and the good luck of "meeting girls from home."

Walter allowed Bess and Belle to pass to the chairs beyond Miss Blake and thus placed himself beside the not any too desirable spinster.

He made a wry face aside to Jack. He liked girls but the elder Miss Blake!

"Mabel is going to sing 'Dreams,'" she said sweetly. "I do love Mabel's voice in 'Dreams.'"

"Yes, I think I should too," said Walter, but the joke was lost on Jeannette. "Who is that dark man over there?" he asked.

"Oh that's a foreigner. They call him Jones, but that's because his name is so unpronounceable. Isn't he handsome?" asked the lady.

"Rather odd looking I should say," returned Walter, "but it seems to me he is attracted in this direction. Why should he stare over this way so?"

"He knows me," replied Miss Blake, bowing vigorously to "Jones" who was almost turned around in his chair in his determination to see the Chelton party.

"He's mighty rude, I think," Walter complained again, leaning over to speak to Cora who was just beyond Bess. "Do you feel the draft from that window, Cora?" he asked.

"Oh I - " then she stopped. Something in Walter's voice told her that it was not the window draft he was referring to. She glanced across the room, and her eyes fell upon the man she had met at Jim Peter's landing place.

"I think those seats over there - up near the stage are much pleasanter," said Jack, who also saw that something was wrong. "Suppose we change?"

"All right" assented Cora, taking the cue. "There are just four."

"I will stay here with Hazel, while you and Wallie go over there with the girls," suggested Jack. "And say Wallie," he whispered, "if I catch you fanning that young lady in the row ahead I'll - duck you on the way home."

Walter apologized profusely for leaving Miss Blake. She evidently was sorry that the window had been open for she was "so enjoying talking of dear old Chelton." The place had only been thus mentioned by herself.

"Who is that dark man?" Hazel inquired of Jack, for, as if his eyes were magnets, every girl in the group felt they were riveted upon her.

"I don't know," replied Jack, "but he seems to be very much interested in someone here. There, he is watching Cora. I wonder who the fellow is?"

The curtain rising interrupted the speculation. A man cushioned like a cozy corner laughed at himself while waiting for his audience to do so. Then he gave a yell and started to sing a ridiculous song about the milkmaid and the summer boarder. When he had finished one verse he took another "fit" of laughter, but somehow the audience did not see it his way, and when he tried it again, he broke off with an explanation. He felt sure that the people did not quite understand the joke, and he tried to tell them how very funny it was. To relieve the situation another person came on. One side of the figure was draped in the evening garb of a lady, while the other wore the full dress suit of a gentleman. The illusion was not at all bad, especially when the "person" waltzed with himself, with his arms around the other side of the evening dress the effect was really funny.

"That's Spencer," declared Jack to Hazel. "He did that at college. Isn't it great?"

"Very funny," admitted Hazel, while the man made in halves bowed on one side first, then on the other, to his applause.

"Mabel is going to sing now," announced Miss Blake getting a firmer hold on her chair. "I just love to hear Mabel sing."

Jack said he did also, then outside the dropped curtain stepped Mabel.

She was pretty, a little thing with brown eyes and brown hair. She wore the most babyish dress made in empire, and it was evident she knew something about making up for good effect on the stage.

Applause instantly greeted Mabel, and Jack was not the one who first tired of clapping his hands. This pleased Miss Jeannette immensely, and she did not fail to express her pleasure to those about her.

The dark man in the seat across the aisle glanced first at the stage and then at the seat where the elderly lady sat. Jack was watching him, and noted his peculiar glances. Presently Mabel started to sing. Her voice was sweet, and her stage manners attractive.

"Isn't she lovely!" exclaimed Bess to Ed. "I do believe she is studying for the stage."

"Shouldn't wonder," replied the young man under his breath. Then the girl finished the song and bowed with such pretty piquancy that everybody demanded more of her talent.

Jack was still watching the dark man. As the girl left the platform the latter left his seat and went outside of the pavilion.

Presently a messenger tapped Miss Blake on the shoulder, "Your niece wishes to speak to you," the boy said, and at that Jeanette Blake also left her seat and the room.

"Something mysterious about that," said Jack to Hazel, "and I propose seeing it out if I can. I will take you over to the others, and run outside."

Just as he said that, a boy appeared on the platform and

announced that owing to an important message Miss Blake was obliged to leave the hall and could not accommodate with her second number, but that some one else would try to fill her place.

A murmur of dissent arose from the audience.

"How could she get an important message here," Cora asked Ed. "Where in the world could it come from?"

Jack pushed a chair for Hazel in line with the others.

"I am going outside for a moment," he said. "Take care of the girls until I come back."

"All right," agreed the other young men.

"But don't run after Mabel," put in Walter with a laugh.

But that was exactly what Jack Kimball did.

CHAPTER X

MYSTERY UPON MYSTERY

Cora, healthy though she was, did not sleep well that night. Jack did not return to the hall, and had left word with the doorkeeper that he could not get back in time to see his sister but would run up from his bungalow early the next morning. It was early now, and next morning, but Jack had not kept his word.

No one but Cora and Hazel had any idea that this might mean anything important.

"It was so strange, the way that man acted," said Hazel to Cora, as the two made their way to the spring for fresh water. "First he watched you, then when Mabel Blake appeared he kept his eye on her. And such eyes! I believe he could hypnotize any one."

"I hope he did not hypnotize Mabel," replied Cora.

"Or Jack," added Hazel.

"No fear of the latter," declared the sister. "Jack is too level-headed to take any cue in that direction."

"That's just the way I feel about Paul," spoke Hazel. "Isn't it lovely to have such splendid brothers?"

Margaret Penrose

"Nothing could be more satisfactory," declared Cora, "unless it would be having a sister besides. I have often wondered what I should have done if I had not had such splendid girl friends. Do you feel as if a sister would have made your life more complete?"

"I have never thought of it," said Hazel.

"But Cora! Look at that woman!"

Almost creeping through the tall grass the form of a woman could be distinguished. She had evidently come from a boat that was lying along shore - a rowboat. Seeing the girls, the woman stood up.

"It's Kate Simpson!" exclaimed Cora, "and she seems to be looking for our camp!"

"Miss!" called the woman, her voice shaking. "Wait, wait for poor Kate! Oh! I'm droppin' down!"

"What is it, Kate?" asked Cora kindly. "You seem exhausted."

"Oh, indeed I am that," replied the woman, brushing the straggling hair from her forehead. "I am all but dead!"

"What has happened?" asked Cora further.

"I can't tell you here. They might find me, and they'd know the boat."

"We can hide the boat in the bushes, and you may come up to the camp," suggested Cora. "That boat is not hard to lift."

"If you only could, but I'm too done up to help," faltered the woman.

Cora and Hazel easily shifted the light canoe up into the deep grass. Kate got on her feet again, and, following the girls, all made their way to a spot entirely closed in with heavy hemlock trees.

"We may talk here," suggested Cora. "This is what we call our annex - the annex to our camp."

"It's better than the shack I've been living in," murmured the woman. "I'm done with that. Here," and she slipped her hand in her dress, carefully taking from a patched place in her skirt a small article. "This is yours - I know it!"

"My ring!"

Cora's eyes sparkled akin to the gem at which she was gazing. Hazel looked on dumbfounded.

"Yes, it's your ring, but don't ask me how I got it," said Kate, "though I'm pretty sure you can guess."

"I knew who had it, and I felt I would get it back," Cora replied, "but I never dreamed how I might recover it. Mother gave it to me on my last birthday."

"Well I'll tell you this much, miss," and Kate Simpson glanced furtively around her, to make sure that no one might be approaching. "If there ever was two bigger villains than Jim Peters and Tony whatever-his-other-name-is-if-he's-got one, then I never heard tell of them. They're up to some new trick every day and another new one every night. But the worst -"

She seemed afraid to go on. Evidently even a woman so used to hardship as this one could be frightened.

"The worst?" asked Cora.

"Is the one that goes on at Fern Island," almost whispered the strange creature.

"Goes on?" exclaimed Hazel, who had hitherto been silent, too interested to interrupt.

"Yes, miss, it goes on, and it will go on I'm afraid while them villains live."

There was a shout from the camp. The others were looking for Hazel and Cora. The familiar yodel was sent back, then Cora told Hazel:

"You run over, Hazel, and do something to interest them, while I take Kate up the back way. I want to get her some of those things the last maid left, and I want to refresh her a little."

"But I couldn't wait, dear," sighed Kate. "If I don't get a train or boat away from this place soon, they'll be sure to catch me."

"But you have done nothing wrong! Why shouldn't you go or come as you want to?" asked Cora.

"I can't tell you, miss, but them men seem to have some power and I want to get away from it. Where might I find a train or a boat?"

"If you have to go, I'll take you to the landing in my motor boat," replied Cora. "It has a canopy and you will not be seen on the water."

"If you could. I'd be very thankful. You see I'm not much used to the water, and rowing over from the shack nearly did me up."

"But I want to give you something for getting me my ring," insisted Cora. "It is quite valuable, you know."

"I heard them say so, and now that the other girl is gone I'll tell you this much. Never you go over to that shack again," and the woman raised a warning finger. "It was a good thing you met me instead of Jim Peters the day you did go over.

They'll be like tigers when they find I've got the ring. It was last night that gave me the chance. They had been out very late, and Tony didn't have any letters to copy so he fell asleep and - and I slipped away with it. I slept a bit under a tree, but indeed I was glad to see daylight."

"And you have been out all night? You must not think of taking a journey without first having something to eat. If you are afraid to come up to camp I'll have something put in the boat for you," declared Cora. "But let me ask you, did you overhear anything about a girl named Miss Blake? I saw Jones leave a hall where she was singing last night, and I suspect he met her as she went out. My brother followed, but I have not seen him since. He stops at the boys' camp," Cora explained.

"Blake? So that was the pretty girl who sang. Well, she had better be careful that she doesn't join the ghosts at Fern Island," said the woman, mysteriously.

"I know the girl. She's from my home place. And that is why my brother went to see that nothing happened to her," Cora said.

"Well, you are good people, one can see that," declared Kate. "But wait. I can't read much, but I picked this up to wrap the ring in."

She handed Cora a soiled and crumpled telegram blank. Upon it was made out, in message form, these words:

"Can place your friend at twenty-five week. Answer at once."

BENEDICT.

Cora pondered for a moment. "Who could have sent Jones such a message?" she asked.

"Sent it?" repeated Kate. "He sends his own messages. He can copy any handwriting. I heard him say the trick worked," she finished.

The truth flashed into Cora's mind. That man somehow knew the Blakes. He was pretending to place little vain Mabel with some theatrical company. When he left the Casino it was to show her the bogus message. And Jack must have been somewhere around within hearing distance. Surely things were getting complicated and mysterious in the summer colony. But Cora had her ring back, and for the rest she felt certain that the "ghost" of Fern Island, also the wild looking girl of whom they had gotten a glimpse, were in some way being wronged by Jim Peters and his associate, the handwriting expert.

CHAPTER XI

THE RACES

"Of course we will enter," declared Cora. "I know my boat and I think it is as good as any little motor craft on the water."

"But suppose we should get stuck away out in the lake," objected Bess. "Then what would we do?"

The girls and boys were talking together a few days after Cora had helped mysterious Kate to get away, and had entered the water contest.

"There would be plenty of boats to give us a tow," replied Cora, "but I have not the slightest idea of getting stuck. My engine works splendidly."

She found an opportunity to whisper to her brother: "What about Miss Blake?"

"I'll tell you later, sis," he whispered back. "It isn't very important. Don't ask me now," and then he went on fussing over the engine and oil cups.

"If we only had our canoe," wailed Jack.

"That was different from any boat I have seen here. It was built on racing lines. Funny what became of it."

Margaret Penrose

"Funny?" repeated Ed. "Tragic I think!" and he gave his sleeves another upward turn just to be doing something.

"Deplorable," added Walter. "I think I looked just sweet in that canoe. Don't you, Hazel?"

"Well, when I saw you - you did," she admitted, "but three boys in a canoe are not quite as attractive -"

"As one girl and one boy," he put in. "Well, that is my own opinion, but Jack and Ed are so inartistic. I never can get them to see things my way."

"We will race in the Peter Pan," Ed announced. "Of course she cannot be beaten. But it is not half as much fun to depend upon an engine as to rely upon muscle. The canoe for me."

"But the glory!" exclaimed Belle. "That boat is beautiful."

"The boat is! Look at us," and Jack stood almost on his head. "Boats are all right, but in the beauty class we come first."

"What time do they start?" Cora inquired. "I've forgotten."

"Motors at three, smaller craft earlier. I am going over to the Point to see the hand-boats," said Jack. "Of course everybody is interested in them."

"Then girls," advised Cora, "get ready. We will have an early lunch, and go out for the afternoon. Perhaps we will bring the cup back."

"Lucky if you bring your boat back," Jack cautioned. "Don't you want me to look the engine over, Cora?"

"No, indeed. That would be a dangerous thing to do, for I now have every part clear. I have put on a bigger oil cup, have had the water circulation increased so the engine can not heat so, I have had a throttle control put up at the steering wheel so that I can slow down from there, and I tell you, Jackie, I have worked out the secrets of that engine until there are no more."

"I should say you had, sis. I never knew there were so many attachments. Well, I know I can depend upon you to keep up the honor of the Kimball family. Come along fellows. Let's see that the Peter Pan is not done by the 'Peter Petrel.' I noticed she was puffing out a lot of oil this morning as we came over."

"Then," said Cora, "you want to be careful. Your oil will run out and the best engine made will stop short if that happens."

"Whew!" exclaimed Ed. "Suppose we get Cora to look over our boat? She seems to know."

"Better have Paul do it," suggested Cora. "That boat is worth three thousand dollars, and I wonder they ever allowed you boys to rent it."

"They would not if Paul had not vouched for them," Hazel explained. "They have a great regard for Paul's skill."

"And is he not going in the races?" asked Bess.

"I haven't heard him say," replied the sister.

"Bet he'll be a dark horse," suggested Ed. "Well, we can't wish Paul any too much good luck, but I do wish he would not stick so dose to his boats and tools. We scarcely see anything of him."

"Nor do I," agreed Hazel with a sigh. "I miss him dreadfully."

"Poor child," and Walter affected to put his big brown arm around the girl. "Let me make up for Paul. Does he kiss you very often?" and he brushed her cheek.

"Walter Pennington!" gasped the circumspect Hazel, "Do have sense!"

"That's what Cora taught me - to help the needy," he floundered.

"Come now, no more nonsense," ordered Cora. "If we are to race we have to get ready." A few hours later Cedar Lake was alive with craft. The rowboats and canoes were lined up first and our friends from Chelton, the girls in the Petrel and the boys in the Peter Pan, kept a sharp look out for the lost canoe. Of course they knew it would be repainted, but the lines being different from those of other boats they hoped to be able to distinguish it, should it appear for the races.

The judges had taken their places. The platform at the Point was gaily decorated for the occasion, and all sorts of banners were flying. The course was to cover one mile, and it ran clear out into the open lake so that the delightful view was unobstructed.

Of all the canoes a bright red craft with a girl in Indian garb attracted most attention. The girl had her hair flying and was indeed a striking figure in the brilliant bark.

There were many green boats, all having Indian names, and there were those of wood in the natural color. Girls vied with boys in point of numbers, and had it all their own way in point of attractiveness.

"They are all ready," Cora told her friends, as the man on the bench who held the pistol allowed it to glimmer in the sunlight. The next moment a crack rent the air and the boats shot off.

For some moments no one spoke. All attention was riveted on the graceful canoes that so motionlessly covered the deep blue lake. The dip of the paddles was the only sign of movement although the dainty boats were making good time in covering the courses. Suddenly when all others had left and were off a light canoe shot out from some place, and a girl with her hair flying, and dressed most peculiarly, started off after them all.

"She gave them a handicap," said Cora, then something occurred to her. The same thought came to the others for each held her breath.

"The ghost girl!" whispered Belle, finally. "However did she get in?"

"It surely is! See her go! And there - there is that man from Peters'," exclaimed Bess to Cora, "and he, too, is in the race."

"They can beat anything on the lake," declared Hazel. "See her go!"

"See him go!"

In a few seconds those who had so mysteriously entered, the race were far up in the line with those who had first started. The girl was wonderfully graceful, and the man showed marked skill at the paddle. He was trying to keep close to her, that was evident, but at a cheer from the shore and from the outlying boats the girl shot ahead and was soon out of hearing of the man, who evidently was her companion.

"She will beat him - she will beat them all!" declared Cora, and this was the opinion of most of the thousands of spectators.

"But if she does," faltered Belle, "do you suppose she will go to the stand dressed like that to receive the prize?"

"We shall see," said Cora. "At any rate this combination is far more interesting than the real race."

A red canoe was alongside the girl in the light one. For a few moments it seemed she would be outdone. Then, with a clever light dip of her paddle, that scarcely seemed to touch the water, the Fern Island girl was again ahead.

The first course had been covered and the boats were turned back for the final run.

"The man has dropped out," said Belle, "See there he is just floating along."

"He wouldn't be beaten, I suppose," Cora surmised, "Any one could see that the girl would come in first."

"They are coming back and she has not started," said Belle, who had the marine glasses.

"But she will," declared Cora.

"Yes, there she comes! Oh isn't it exciting! To have the queer girl beat all those who pride themselves on their skill. I wonder who or what she can be?" queried Hazel.

"Here come our boys," said Belle, as the beautiful golden Peter Pan motored over to the smaller Petrel.

"What do you think of that?" called Jack. "Look at the Wild Duck!"

"Isn't she a - bird!" confirmed the voice of Ed.

"A Sea Gull," added the more polite Walter. "I say, girls, do you happen to know her?"

"Yes," called back Cora, "We have met her."

Then there was an exchange of words understandable only to those expressing them, and to those for whom they were expressed, but any one might have guessed that the boys in the Peter Pan were asking the girls in the Petrel to let them "meet" the wild bird of the light canoe.

"They are almost in," said Bess, breathlessly. "Oh I hope she does not back out."

"No danger," said Cora. "One can see that she is making for the finish line."

"There are two boys who have been saving themselves," Hazel remarked. "I shouldn't wonder if they could beat our friend."

"Oh, I hope not," exclaimed Belle. "I should be so disappointed."

"And it would be impolite of them," added the innocent Bess, whereat every one laughed.

The boys had been saving their strength. Now they paddled off and their craft, one of brown and one green, seemed equal to any of the others.

"Hello there!" called Jack. "Did you notice?"

"What?" asked Cora.

"The canoe - the Gerkin?"

"He means it has lines like the lost boat," said Cora. "I have not seen it enough to know," she finished, but at the same time she took the glasses to look at the new rival of the wild girl.

"Yes it has, I remember," said Bess. "I had a good look at it the afternoon that they lost it. I was waiting for you to fix up your boat Cora, and I saw the boys' canoe."

"Well, I suppose they could never be certain, as there must be more than one boat built even on those lines," said Cora. "My! See how close they are - the girl and the boys!"

"She's ahead!" exclaimed Belle, clapping her hands. "How I hope she wins!"

"We all do!" declared Hazel.

Then they were silent. The first canoe was almost in, and it was the one called the Gerkin, paddled by the boys.

"Go it girl!" screamed the boys from the Peter Pan.

"Beat them, girlie!" called the girls from the Petrel.

For one brief second the wild-looking girl turned in the direction from which the voices had come. Hats were waved to her, handkerchiefs flaunted and then she paddled - paddled straight ahead and came into the finish first!

"Hurrah! Hurrah!" went up shout after shout.

"I knew it!" cried Cora joyously. "Now let us watch her."

"There's that dark man!" Bess told them. "Oh! I just wish he would keep away from her."

But he did not. The girl in the light canoe turned from the spectators as if she had been deaf and dumb. And it was the dark man - the fellow called Tony Jones - who went up to the judges to get their verdict.

CHAPTER XII

ONE WAY TO WIN

"We have no time now," Jack told Cora, "but as soon as the races are over I will ask what that fellow told the judges. Certainly he must have said that he had a right to, the girl's prize, or they would not have given it to him."

"But how the poor thing hurried off! Why, she hardly had a chance to know that she won," replied the sister. "I think it a shame that the creature should be treated like something really wild," and she turned to watch the foamy wake that the little canoe was tracing, as the girl from Fern Island hurried to hide herself again where ever she might go. The signal precluded the possibility of further interest just then in the strange case, but indeed Cora's mind was not so readily shifted. She wanted to know about that girl.

The speed boats were next to be tried out. What a splendid showing! Who would have dreamed that such handsome craft were on the waters of Cedar Lake? Of course they were all private boats, and their flags flaunted proudly before the spellbound spectators.

The Peter Pan was among the very finest. In this were our boy friends from Chelton, and as they lined up the admiration expressed was unstinted. The Sprint was another splendid speed boat, built with torpedo stern and a queer spray hood at the bow. This was being run by a girl - a young lady noted for

Margaret Penrose

her skill at any sort of motor.

"Oh, I hope our boys win," exclaimed Bess, as if that hope needed to be made known.

"They have a good chance," argued Cora. "Of course so many things may happen that there is absolutely no surety of any machinery on the water." She looked to see that the oil cup levers of the Petrel were down to prevent the lubricant flowing before it was needed and also gave a critical survey of the little wire that connected on the cylinder. It emitted a clear "fat" spark as she touched it to the metal, and this seemed to satisfy her.

"I guess ours is all right; isn't it?" asked Hazel. "Wouldn't it be fine if we won something!"

"I fully intend to," declared Cora.

"That means that we will," responded Belle. "If Cora intends!"

"They're off!" called out Hazel, "look at Jack!"

He was standing over the engine evidently making sure that even at the start he should not loose a single atom of the power that twirled the propeller. Ed was at the steering wheel. Walter was at the side, and with him was Paul Hastings.

"There's Paul!" exclaimed Bess, when they could make out that the fourth figure in the boat was that of the boy's friend. "I thought he would run another boat."

"He wouldn't want any other to beat the Peter Pan," explained Hazel, "and at the same time he would not take the glory of it from the boys who have it for the season. That's Paul," she finished proudly.

The first "leg" of the course had been covered, and the three best boats, the Peter Pan, the Sprint, and the Lady B. were all in line. A dozen others were trailing, and while they showed less speed it was not safe to say that they could not catch up with the three stars. From buoy to buoy over the triangular course the boats fairly shot, and a beautiful sight they made on the green-hilled basin of Cedar Lake.

The course was covered once and then the second round was started by the boats that had qualified. These were only five in number, one of them being a very queer looking craft, built high on the sides like a huge box and showing at the bow a double point, like a pair of slippers. This of course attracted considerable attention, and it shot past the Sprint, which was run by the young lady who had hoped to meet with no rival such as a home-made boat, to say the least.

"Can't that go? Look at it!" the spectators were exclaiming.

"See, Paul is at the Peter Pan's engine!" said Cora, as the color of that boy's cap made it plain that he had taken Jack's place. "I hope Jack has not strained his wrist, or done anything like that."

"Very likely Paul is just seeing if everything is right," said Hazel. "See, there, Jack has his place again."

During the second and third trials all interest was centered on the Peter Pan, the Hague, (the home-made boat), and the Sprint. Now this would be ahead, and now that, until it seemed that there could be but little difference in the merits of any of the three. Of course most of the sympathy was with the Sprint, because a girl was striving to outdo the boys. At the same time, the Hague, being such an oddity, and the lake folks knowing that this had been built by the boys who were running it, came in for its share of applause.

"There is not a boat on the lake that can fairly beat the Peter Pan," Hazel declared almost feverishly, for the others were threatening to do so. "I have heard Paul say so."

"He ought to know," said Cora with a sly wink, "but that big tub, the Hague, is something new. Perhaps it has the power of a destroyer."

"It is big and clumsy enough to have any sort of power," remarked Belle. "I should just be sick if it did win."

"All's fair, in a fair race," remarked Cora. "See the Hague is ahead!"

One more course was to be made, and every eye and every mind was centered on this, the final test.

The Peter Pan shot out bravely and safely. The Sprint made a splendid second! Then the Hague! Something seemed wrong. It was "missing." That could plainly be heard from the girl's boat. Away they flew, yard after yard being made in wonderfully short time. The Sprint was doing well with the Peter Pan. The Hague suddenly shot forward, passed every thing - passed the Sprint - passed the Peter Pan and won!

"Hurrah for the tub!" yelled the crowd. "Hurrah for home talent!" shouted the throng. But the young lady in the Sprint throttled down and her boat drifted over to the boys.

"How was that?" she asked breathlessly.

"I don't know," replied Paul "but I'm going to find out. We were second and you made a splendid run - but I'm going to look into the glories of the Tub!"

So keen was the disappointment of the girls in the Petrel that they seem to have lost heart for their own race, which came next. But when Ed and Jack called out to them, and Paul waved his cap in his own quiet way, the encouragement dispelled their lost of interest.

Cora spun the flywheel, and the boat took its place. She looked every inch a girl to win, while Hazel kept close to the steering wheel and the twins did their part in just looking pretty. The motor girls' boat was the cynosure of every eye, as it happened to be the only boat in that class run by girls.

The signal was given and they started off.

"Steady!" Jack called. "Go it, sis!"

He should hardly have done this, but his boyish love for the girls and their boat could not be restrained. Then they waved, and the maroon and white flag stood out tense and defiant like some animate thing.

Not a word was spoken by the girls. It seemed so important to pay all attention to the machine upon which depended the loss or gain of a victory - if we may say that a victory can be lost.

"Look out!" called Hazel suddenly and a boat crossed their path so closely that Cora was obliged to throttle down, and Hazel had to run straight for a buoy to avoid a collision, and the craft hit the course marker. Then the Petrel stopped short! It simply wouldn't move!

"Oh!" sighed Belle and Bess in one voice, but Cora jumped up and tried for a spark. None came!

She looked at the connections. They seemed all right.

"Maybe it's in the gas," she said nervously, while the other boats were passing them by.

She yanked down the bulkhead board that hid the gasoline tank. Then she saw the cause of the trouble.

"Short circuited!" she exclaimed. "That happened when we struck the buoy. It jarred the battery wires together," and the next instant she had adjusted the difficulty and the engine, glad to be off again, seemed to try to make up for the lost seconds.

Every one in the Petrel breathed a sigh of relief. The anxiety had been intense.

"I was certainly afraid we would have to row to shore," Belle said, taking a more comfortable position.

"We will make up for it," declared Cora, throwing on full speed and directing Hazel as to the best way to hold the wheel exactly straight and in doing so to get all possible distance out of each explosion of the engine.

They finished in a tie over the first course. This was encouraging, for the little Mischief, their closest opponent, was acknowledged a fine boat.

Two more courses were to finish the race, unless there was another tie. The girls scarcely noticed the frantic efforts of the boys in the Peter Pan who were encouraging and directing at the top of their lungs. The young men in the Mischief were anxious. They could never stand it to be beaten by a couple of country girls! But, on the second trial Cora's boat won, and then came the final test.

Up the lake they went again! Now the Petrel was ahead and now the Mischief until the closeness of the two became absorbing.

"The best race of the day!" the judges were declaring. "Neither has it all her own way!"

"Plucky girls," said another of the men at the stand. "Whatever happened when they stopped they must have been well able to handle, from the way they caught up again. I thought they were out of it that time!"

"We all did," put in some one else, "but I have seen that little girl on the lake before. She knows something about a motor boat."

"Here they come!" Jack yelled. "Just look at Cora! Isn't she fine!"

"And Hazel!" put in Paul with a smile.

"How about Bess and Belle?" asked the fickle Walter. "I think they look just sweet!"

Only two more "legs," and the Petrel was still ahead!

One was covered, with the Mischief so close that only those in the best position could tell which one led.

"Steady, Hazel!" cautioned Cora. Straight as an arrow she directed the wheel.

Then there was a splash from a nearby motor boat. A shout and screams!

"Overboard!" yelled the frantic onlookers. "A child overboard!"

It was just at the side of the Petrel!

"Hazel! The engine! Bess, the wheel!" shouted Cora, and before any one knew what she was about, she had jumped into the water and was making for the spot were the child had gone under.

The boys in the Mischief did not stop. Hazel took the engine and Bess the wheel, realizing that Cora meant for them to finish.

Presently she came up with the child in her arms!

"Go it, girls!" she called, "Win! Win!"

The Mischief was close alongside. Cora was clinging to the side of the boat from which the child had dropped, while the almost fainting mother was recovering her little one. The others assisted Cora in, and forgot all about her race.

But Cora stood spellbound in the cockpit, dripping wet. She stood there ignoring the thanks poured out on her.

"Steady, Hazel!" she called. "Win - win for me!"

That was enough. The motor girls, those in the Petrel, realizing that their leader was safe, now determined to "win for her."

The Mischief had gained in the time that Cora swung overboard, and now was just abreast of the Petrel. The slight change of course also told in the last few yards, but now Hazel and Bess forgot everything but the call of Cora to win, and their boat, like a flash, sprang up to its opponent and passed it by the closest record made in any of the races.

"Hurrah! Hurrah!" rang out in their ears.

"A double victory!" shouted one of the judges. Then the Petrel was turned back to get Cora who was in the other motor boat.

The boys in the Peter Pan had not seen Cora dive over for the child, but as quickly as they heard the report, that was now being spread about, they made for the boat from which the accident occurred.

Back with them went the boat of the accident crew, and when Cora finally returned to her own craft she had an escort of honor to the judges stand.

"First prize for the Petrel!" announced the head judge. "And the honor medal for life-saving to Miss Cora Kimball, the leader of our brave little crew of motor girls."

CHAPTER XIII

VICTORS AND SPOILS

"Wasn't it exciting!" Belle was saying to the little party that had gathered around Cora as she received their praise and congratulations after it was all over. "I never dreamed that boat races could furnish so many kinds of excitement."

"I don't call it all delightful," objected Bess putting her arms around the still wet form of the girl who had made the rescue, "and I don't want to see Cora jump overboard that way again. I shall never forget it."

"A good way to find out how much folks think of me" replied Cora. "I really didn't mind it a bit, once I knew that I could get the child before she got under a boat. That was all that worried me."

"Your cup is a beauty though, sis," said Jack, who was examining the trophy. "I think it's prettier than the one we lost. Paul is not satisfied that we lost fairly though, and he's up there now disputing it."

"What good can that do now?" asked Belle.

"No telling. Paul knows what he is about," replied Jack. "But say, did you know that the wild girl in the canoe is deaf and dumb?"

Margaret Penrose

"No!" exclaimed all the girls in one voice.

"Yes that's what the dark fellow who was trailing her told the judges, and that is why, I guess, she scampered off so. Too bad! She is pretty too."

"And did the man take her prize?" asked Cora.

"Sure thing," replied the brother. "He said he was her guardian."

Cora thought for a moment. "Seems to me," she said finally, "that she turned towards us when we shouted to her."

"Sometimes deaf people know such things by instinct," Jack offered as an explanation. "I thought too, that she gave us a knowing glance."

"Pure conceit," said Ed. "Wallie claimed the glance, but I saw her hair float in my direction."

"She's a star canoeist," declared Jack, "and I should like to be better acquainted with her."

"Can you talk with your fingers?" asked Belle. "I know a little of the sign language, but I would not be too sure that I could carry on a conversation."

"But you could introduce one," insisted Jack, "and once she knew I wanted to know her - I might depend upon - true love to make known all the rest."

"Here! Here! Jackie!" cautioned Cora, "you are not to talk of love - until mother comes home. You have promised to look after me."

"As if Ed and Walter couldn't do that ten times better than I can. But hello! Here comes Paul - the Paul."

"It's ours," called Paul, before he was dose enough to talk in the regulation tones. "Come on up! The judges want to see the crew of the Peter Pan!"

"Ours!" echoed Jack, Ed and Walter.

"It certainly is ours. Those fellows had the gasoline doped?"

"What's that?" asked Ed.

"They had camphor and some other stuff in their gas," went on Paul, "and the engine nearly kicked out of the boat."

"Did they admit it?" inquired Ed.

"Not until I charged them with it," replied Paul. "I knew there was something up when they got ahead on that jump. Then I asked if I might take a look at that freak engine, and they allowed me to do so. I smelled camphor the minute I stepped aboard. They even had not sense enough to hide the bottle, and it's against the present racing rules on this lake to doctor gas. So I taxed them with it, and they finally admitted it and we went together to the judges. They were pretty decent chaps and did not seem to mind, very much, relinquishing the prize. You know what it is, don't you?"

"Certainly, it's a dandy canoe," said Jack, "And you really mean that it is to be ours?"

"If you don't hurry along some one else may claim it," said Paul. "It isn't mine, it's yours."

"And to think that we and our boys both got prizes!" exclaimed Hazel. "Isn't it too good to be true?"

"And too good to be false," answered Paul. "Now, boys, let's run along. I have something to do before evening."

"And I had better make for camp," said Cora. "These togs

are wet."

"Of course," said Belle with sympathy in her voice. "But when do you get your medal, Cora?"

"I believe it comes from Philadelphia. Some wealthy man has it stored there waiting to be claimed."

"It's a wonder the mother of that little girl didn't want to adopt you, Cora," said Jack, as the boys started off with Paul. "I thought from the way she hung on to you she had intentions. Well, so long. We will give you first ride in our new canoe, and let us hope we will have better luck with this one than we had with the other," and then the boys went off for the prize.

"I can't get over that girl being deaf and dumb," said Hazel, as the girls made their way to the camp. "I can scarcely believe it."

"Well, now we have a double interest on Fern Island," Cora answered. "If there is really such an unfortunate creature hid or hiding there she ought to be rescued. I cannot understand, either, how that foreigner can be her guardian."

"That Jones?" asked Bess, as innocently as if she had not seen the girl race and heard about the man claiming her prize.

"Why, yes, of course," replied Cora. "And he says she is deaf and dumb. Who's calling? Didn't you hear some one?"

"Yes, there's Mabel Blake hurrying after us," said Belle. "She looks excited."

The girl who was running along the path did indeed "look excited." The motor girls waited.

"Oh, I thought I would never catch up to you!" Mabel panted. "You do walk at such a pace!"

"Why, how are you, Mabel?" asked Cora graciously. "I heard you had gone back to Chelton."

"We did intend to - but we haven't," she faltered. "Jeannette has been ill."

"Ill!" exclaimed more than one voice.

"Yes, that's what I want to see you about. I don't know what to do," and Mabel's pretty brown eyes filled to the lashes.

"Can we help you?" Cora asked.

"I would like to speak with you alone, Cora," she said. "But I know what you did this afternoon, and I see you have still to change your clothing."

"They are almost dry now," Cora replied. "Yet if you could wait five minutes I could easily change in that time. Here we are. Home again. And there! Nettie has heard all about our victories; haven't you Nettie?"

"Indeed yes, Miss Cora. But I was afraid for you," replied the maid. "The child's father sent a message up here to ask when he might see you?"

"Oh, they make too much fuss over a trifle," replied Cora. "Sit here on the porch with the girls, Mabel. I will be out soon."

Finally Mabel pressed her handkerchief to her eyes and murmuring some sort of unintelligible excuse she rushed indoors.

She was met in the hall by Cora.

"Why, what is it, Mabel?" she asked, putting her arms about the sobbing one.

"Oh, I cannot stand it," wailed Mabel. "The disgrace!"

"What disgrace?"

"The - that - man!" she stammered. "But I must go back to Jeannette. I am afraid she is losing her mind. Of course, you could not go with me, Cora. It would be too much after your hard afternoon. But Jeannette got your letter."

"Yes? I hope she understood it."

Mabel tried to dry her eyes. "I suppose she did if any one could understand such a thing," she replied. "But to think it is in the Chelton paper!"

"When was it in?" Cora asked.

"It will be out to-morrow!" replied the tearful one.

"To-morrow," Cora repeated thoughtfully. "Perhaps Jack could stop it. He is well acquainted with the editor."

"Oh, if he only could," and Mabel brightened up. "That's what makes Jeannette feel so dreadfully."

"It was very unfortunate," Cora said. "He is a dangerous man."

"Dangerous! I think he should he put in jail," declared Mabel hotly.

"But it is so difficult to catch such people," Cora remarked. "You could scarcely name your charge against him?"

"Name it? Never!" exclaimed the girl.

"There you are. One woman who might put him in jail flies off to New York. You could at least accuse him of fraud and you refuse. I myself know of one wrong doing that affected me and I prefer to keep quiet - for the present at least. You see what cowards we all are where our pride is concerned.

"You are not a coward, Cora Kimball," exclaimed Mabel, "and I know perfectly well you would denounce him if you thought that safest."

"At any rate, Mabel, I think it will all come out right," Cora assured her. "Just wait until I have a glass of milk and I will go over and see Jeannette."

"I can never tell how it all happened," sighed Mabel, "I really think he had me hypnotized."

"He is a clever rogue," agreed Cora, and she knew now more about his roguery than she cared to sum up even to herself.

CHAPTER XIV

TALKING IT OVER

The interview with Miss Jeannette Blake was not altogether satisfactory, but Cora was too careful of the sick one's feelings to ask deliberate questions. She could not really find out how far the Blakes had gone with Tony Jones in the matter of paying him for the alleged placement of Mabel with a theatrical company, but she guessed they had either actually paid a large sum, or had given a note that might be equally compelling.

Also the notices that had been prepared for the press announcing her coming "debut" were very embarrassing.

It was the day after the races, and Cora sat with her brother on the porch of their bungalow. She had told him of Mabel's plight and was asking him to help her clear up some of the shades and shadows.

"Tell me, Jack," she asked, "what happened the night you followed Mabel out of the pavilion - the night that man gave her the false message?" Jack thrust his hands deep into his pockets, and looked very serious - for him. "To tell the truth, Cora," he began, "I had to make love to Mabel to get her out of his clutches."

"Make love to her, Jack!"

"Nothing smaller would do but you know, sis, the love was only a sort of sample, the kind a fellow might safely give away to any girl."

Cora laughed. "You funny boy," she said, "to flatter a girl to save her from - flattery."

"But didn't you ask me to? Didn't you say to watch Mabel that time you whispered as I was leaving? You are the funny one. It was you that put the wicked plot in my fair young head," and he sighed in mock sincerity.

"But honestly, did you see that man give her the telegram? It seems to me you might be a witness should there be trouble."

Jack jumped up. "Oh, no, you don't, sis!" he declared. "You don't get me in any further mischief. Mabel is too fond of me now."

"Jack, don't be silly! I want you to wire the editor of the Chelton paper that, owing to the sudden illness of Miss Jeannette Blake, her niece, Miss Mabel Blake, has been compelled to stop her musical studies, and postpone her debut as a singer. That is all true and if the other notice does appear you can arrange to have this given as the latest."

"Foxy!" declared jack. "'Not a word of fib and not a grain of truth. Well, you would beat Jones if you went at his game, but I do think it a good idea to wire Nat Phillips. I'll go and do so at once," he added, feeling in his pocket to make sure he had with him change enough to pay for the message.

"And Jack," Cora went on, "since you have been so good, don't you think it would be lovely for you to sort of keep track of Mabel for a day or two? That man, I am afraid, has her under some sort of influence, and there is no telling what he might not try to do to get some Blake money."

"Make more love to her? Suppose she takes me up?"

"I really cannot explain it all, Jack," said Cora gravely, "but the man has frightened more than Mabel. The woman who kept house for him and Peters was so afraid that he would find out she was leaving, that I could scarcely persuade her to wait while I changed the batteries in my boat. She kept saying she wanted to get out of his power. And now Mabel declares he had her hypnotized. Then that sort of queer girl who won the canoe race - surely he has her somehow in his power, as they express it."

"Powerful man," answered Jack, "but how is it, Cora, that you talked with him and he did not hoodoo you?"

"Oh I'm immune I suppose," and she smiled with her handsome face turning up in becoming hauteur.

"Guess Ed thinks that, too," said the brother mischievously. "He has been growling to me about it."

"Ed is a dear, nice boy," she said simply.

"That's the sort of compliment a girl always pays the fellow she is going to turn down," Jack declared.

"I think, brother, making love to Mabel has gone to your head. But hurry along to the station and send off the message."

Cora sat there silent for a few moments. There was no one about the camp but herself, and she would soon go down to the lake for a run in her boat. She was thinking that of all the peculiar cases of other people's troubles in which she felt she had a right to interfere that of the girl who was said to be deaf and dumb and who was probably hidden somewhere on Fern Island was the case most urgent. If only she could really find her, and find that poor demented old man who had so strangely crossed her path. Cora had not the least fear of either of them and suddenly she resolved to go alone to Fern Island and try to find them.

Ten minutes later, when she had left a note dangling from the hanging lamp in the dining room, saying to the girls that she would be back by supper time, Cora was gliding up Cedar Lake in the Petrel.

She was glad that she did not meet any of her friends who would, of course, ask where she was going. And now she was too far away to meet any boats of summer fisher folks or pleasure seekers.

"I am beginning to believe in the psychic," she mused, "for I have a feeling that a cry for help comes from that perfectly silent island."

Her heart beat quickly as she throttled down her engine, stopped it, and finally stepped ashore. Her landing was made on a different side of the island than before and she saw instantly that feet had been treading down the ferns from shore to inland. This path served to guide her along. Then she noticed particles of food.

"Hardly picnic folks along here," she thought. "Perhaps the canoe girl is somewhere about -"

But what was her terror when she faced the shore at a dear spot in the woods and against it saw the boat of the man Peters.

"Oh!" she gasped. "He must be on the island!"

Then she listened. Yes, there was a step! She sank down behind a clump of thick bushes and while hiding there she saw, not Peters, but Jones saunter down to the water's edge!

How she trembled! A half-fainting sensation overcame her. From a crouching attitude she sank flat on the ground and felt too weak to attempt to raise herself.

Meanwhile the man had reached his rowboat and pushed off. He glanced along and saw the motor boat.

"That girl!" he muttered. "She is interfering with my plans again. This would be an ideal place for a -" Then he stopped. "Bah! I'll just give her a chance to think over her courage."

Cora was still under the bush, and did not hear the gentle purr of her engine as the man started down Cedar Lake in her own precious motor boat, dragging his rowboat behind.

CHAPTER XV

TWO GIRLS ON THE ISLE

"He's gone!" Cora murmured, as creeping out from her hiding place, she could see that the rowboat had left the shore. "Well, I am safe again, for I have not the slightest fear of any one who may be on this island - now."

Cora glanced about her in a dazed way. Then she noticed that the bent grass and fern led toward a hill in a deep part of the wood.

"Strange," she was thinking. "I feel so absolutely certain that the young girl is about here, and that she needs help."

The path was so faintly outlined that Cora could scarcely trace it, but she knew if any one was in hiding the place of concealment must be at the end of the path.

Several times she looked back of her to make sure that the man Jones was not following. Then suddenly she thought she heard a faint moan!

She listened. Yes, that was a sob and in a girl's weak voice. Cora quickened her steps, and forgetting now to watch the path she was covering, forgetting all except that a human creature must be in pain, and that she could probably help that person. Cora Kimball almost ran until she reached the hill, where she saw a sort of screen made from the broken branches of trees.

Another moan! It was behind that screen! Quick as a flash Cora jerked down the branches, thrust her head into a cave and there beheld the one who was sobbing and moaning.

It was the canoe girl! She lay on a bed of pine needles her pretty face as pale as death, and her lovely hair tangled in the pine pallet.

As Cora pushed her way into the queer cave, the girl turned, and seeing her, screamed - such a scream as one might expect from the insane. At the same moment the brush was again pushed from the door and there stood the wild man! His white hair and his white beard showed Cora that he was the same person who had so strangely crossed her path in the woods the day she was fern-gathering.

"I want to help you," Cora spoke timidly, while the girl on the ground moaned pitifully.

"Help?" whispered the man, and his voice was as gentle and soft as a woman's. "They have killed my girl," and he knelt down beside the prostrate figure. He kissed her passionately. Then she opened her eyes.

"Father, dear," she murmured, "You must go - quick!"

He kissed her again; then he turned to Cora.

"Young woman," he said gravely, "you must not harm my darling. She is innocent." Then he left the cave.

What could she do? What should she do? This girl was neither deaf nor dumb, and for that Cora was grateful, but if that dangerous man, who had said she was both, should return, and find Cora with her!

"Dear," said Cora gently, "try to trust me. Tell me what I can do for you?"

"Oh, if I could but die!" the girl sobbed, "but there is father!"

Then Cora saw that she was becoming unconscious. Feeling about the half-dark cave place Cora came upon a pail of water. Beside it was a tin cup and this she filled and carried to the sick girl's lips.

"Try to drink," she whispered. "Then if you can stand I will take you to my house in my boat."

The girl did sip some of the water. Again she opened those wonderful eyes and looked at Cora.

"You are kind," she said. "He did not send you?"

"No one sent me, dear, and I promise never to betray you."

"At last," she murmured, "a friend!"

"Yes, a friend," Cora assured her, "and I am going to prove it to you. I saw you one day as we - some girls and myself came to this island. Then I saw you win that splendid race, and since then I have been determined to find you."

"'He made me do it, he made me go in the race," said the girl, "and now he brings this letter."

"What has shocked you so?" Cora asked. "Was it the letter?"

"Yes, he says they are coming for father!"

"Who?" Cora asked, but the girl's face went so white that again she pressed the tin cup to her lips.

"There," Cora went on, "we will talk of nothing now but of what we shall do to make you well again. Could you walk ever so little a distance? To my motor boat?"

"If I could, what then?" asked the girl.

"Then loving hands would bring back the color into your checks, and then the best boys in the world would come to help your father."

"Help father!" she repeated. "But that can never be done. Father is - an outcast!"

"But he has no disease," Cora said, remembering what Kate, had told her was Tony's excuse for going to see a victim of some dreadful disease, who was on Fern Island.

"No, thank God, his body is well, but his soul is sick - so very sick."

"Let me see if you can sit up?" asked Cora. "It will soon be night and we must try to get away."

"It will, be much better to leave him, and return, soon, well and strong enough to comfort him again," Cora said, "than to stay here, and perhaps die."

"You are right," said the stranger getting up on her elbow. "Oh, what it means to speak with a girl again. Heaven must have sent you."

"There, you are up now," spoke Cora quickly, realizing the importance of urging the girl to get up while she felt so inclined. "See, you can stand! There, now you can walk."

"But I must say good-bye to father. Oh! should I leave him?" she sobbed.

"Just for a little while, dear," Cora again assured her. Then the girl put her finger to her mouth and gave a queer whistle.

"I will be outside so he will know that I am better," said the girl. "Father has been so frightened."

The next moment the man appeared again.

"Father," said the girl, "I am going with this friend some place to get well. Should I go?"

"Friend? Yes, she is all of that. Daughter go!" and the man pressed her to his breast.

"And you will be all right? No one will come for you?"

A look of horror swept over his face. "They shall not find me," he faltered, releasing his daughter from the embrace.

"Let me tell you, sir," ventured Cora, "that the man I just saw leave this island is a villain. Don't believe one word he says."

"Villain? Yes! He is that, for he would have carried off my Laurel!"

"Hush father, you showed him that you had more strength than a coward can have. I feel so much better. I am almost cured since this girl has taken my hand."

"My name is Cora Kimball," said our heroine, "and I have a camp at the lower end of the lake. It is there I am taking Laurel."

"And she may come to see me?" almost sobbed the aged man. "My little wild Laurel."

"Yes, indeed, and some day I feel that we may take you, too, away from this island. There, I do not mean anything to harm you. Come, dear, it is growing dark."

"I will leave a branch of laurel to guide you back to me," the man said to his daughter. "When you come, look for it as I shall place it fresh every day."

"Go now, before I go," his daughter urged. "Then I shall feel that you are safe."

He turned, and the girls stood to watch the last of that queer form as it disappeared over the hill. He was going to one of his many woodland haunts.

"Now we may go," said the lonely one. "Poor, dear father!"

"Be brave," urged Cora, as she led her toward the shore. "I am so glad I found you."

"If you had not I feel I should have gone insane. That man was always terrible, but today he wanted to take me away!"

"Once in my little boat and you will almost forget all those terrible things," said Cora. "I left - it - here!"

Then she stopped in dismay, as she saw that the boat was gone!

CHAPTER XVI

A TERRIBLE NIGHT

"The boat is gone!" Cora almost gasped. Then the girl, the sick frail creature, did a remarkable thing - she came to the rescue of the stronger one.

"No matter," she said calmly. "I feel so much better with a girl to speak to, that if you will put up with my strange life for a night, perhaps it will be all right in the morning. There," as Cora showed by her change of color that she felt it would be a risk, "lots of people think sleeping, out of doors is the very best sort of life. Don't you want to try it?"' and her arm stole around Cora's waist.

"Why, of course we can only try, but I am afraid that you will suffer, Laurel. You are very weak," said Cora.

"No, I was only frightened," and she made an effort to show that she did really feel better. "Now, when we go back we must not let father know that we are still on the island."

Cora did not question this. That the girl had a good reason for keeping her presence a secret from her father she felt certain. But to turn back to those woods! And night so near!

"I suppose there is absolutely no way of getting a boat?" Cora questioned.

Margaret Penrose

"Even my canoe is gone. That awful man is to blame," replied the girl.

"Did he take it?" asked Cora.

"When I refused to go with him, he said I might die here," replied Laurel. "That was to get more money from father. Oh, you cannot know how I have wished to speak with some one!" and her big, brown eyes filled with tears.

"And I am so glad I did come," Cora assured her, "even if our first night must be a lonely one. I am used to queer experiences."

"Then I will have no fear in showing you how I have lived here. Of course, it was for father."

They retraced their steps, and in spite of all the assurances that each pledged to the other it was surely lonely.

"Shall we go to your little pine cave?" Cora asked.

"I think it would be better not to," replied Laurel, "for indeed, one never knows what that man might do. He might come back just to frighten me."

"And he saw how ill you were?"

"Oh, most men think girls get ill to order. Very likely he thought I was acting," and the strange girl almost laughed.

"Our folks will be frightened about me," Cora said. "Are there no means of getting away from here?"

"There is not a person on this island that I know of," replied Laurel. "Of course, Brentano took your boat."

"Brentano?" Cora repeated.

"Yes. Did you not know his name?"

"He seems to have a collection of names. One calls him Tony, another Jones, and now it is Brentano."

"But we knew him abroad. That is his name."

Cora wondered, but did not feel inclined to ask further questions then. It was almost dark, and under the pine trees shadows fell in gloomy foreboding.

"Hark!" exclaimed Cora. "I thought I heard an engine!"

They listened. "Yes it is an engine," replied Laurel, "but I am afraid it is over at Far Island."

"Couldn't we shout?"

"I would rather not. You see father wants to stay here," she said hesitatingly.

"You mean if any one came for us they would know we were not alone here?"

"They might suspect. Or they might just happen to see father."

Cora was sorry. She wanted so much to call to the possible passerby, but she saw that the other girl had some very strong motive in wishing to leave the island secretly.

"Do you never go away from here?" she asked.

"Only when I am forced to, as I was the day of the race. He made me race, threatening to expose father if I did not."

"And then he said that you were deaf and dumb," added Cora indignantly.

"I did not mind that at all. In fact it was the easiest way for me to get out of meeting people." Laurel sighed heavily. "I do wonder when our lives will change," she said finally.

"Let us hope very soon," Cora said. "I, of course, do not know your story, but I feel that in some way that man is wronging you."

"Yes, he has been our evil genius ever since he crossed our path. You see father's mind is not entirely clear, and I do not myself know what to believe."

In the distance they could now see the lights of several boats, and behind the great hill that made Far Island look like some strange mountain place, the sun was all but lost in the forest blackness.

"Oh," sighed Laurel suddenly. "I feel faint again."

She sank down before Cora could support her. And they were away from the little hut where the water was! Away from every thing but the pitiless night!

"Oh, how dreadful," moaned Cora. "What shall I do?"

For a long time Laurel lay there so still that Cora feared she might really die. Then at last, she managed to sit up and grasp Cora's hand.

"I have never been ill in my life," she said. "It was all from that shock the day he compelled me to go in the race."

"Then you have every chance of getting perfectly well again," Cora assured her. "If that dreadful man had only left my boat."

"Perhaps in the morning we may be able to go," Laurel said. "Now that I have made up my mind I feel it will be better for father as well as for me, for if anything happened to me I fear he would die."

A light in the distance for a time gave them hope that a boat might be coming to the island, but, like a number of others, it turned toward the pleasure end of the lake.

"I guess we will have to make the best of it for to-night," Cora sighed. "Shall I try to find the hut and get you some food?"

"And you have not eaten! In my misery I forgot you. Of course - there now - I am better, and we will have to make our way to the pine hut. But if that man comes back!" and she shuddered.

"Why does he hold such power over you?" asked Cora, as she put her arm protectingly around her companion. "Does he supply you with your things out here?"

"We supply him," replied the girl bitterly. "He is never satisfied but always demanding more, until father will soon have nothing left."

Cora was mystified but this was no time for the strange story. She must help the girl to the pine hut.

"I believe you are more weak for want of food than from illness," Cora said. "I hope we find something to eat."

"Oh, yes, he brought things, but he should have done so before. I am weak for food."

It was difficult to find the way back now in the darkness, but the two lonely, frightened girls trudged on. At last Laurel was able to feel the stone on the path that gave the clue to her little hut.

"Does Brentano know you?" she asked Cora suddenly.

"I know him. I have been to his shack, and I have heard a lot about him from a housekeeper who left Peters. Do you know he is a handwriting expert?"

"A hand-writing expert!" gasped the girl. "Does that mean he could copy a signature?"

"Perfectly," replied Cora, "but how you tremble? What is it now?"

"Girl! girl!" she gasped. "What that may mean to us! Oh, I must find father! He will know. I must signal to him."

"Please do not to-night," begged Cora, fearing a new collapse from the excitement. "Wait until daylight. Here, now we shall get our food."

They were within the pine hut and had lighted a lantern. A loaf of bread and some salt meat were easy to find in the rudely-made box that served for a closet.

"I am actually starved," Cora remarked, with an effort to be pleasant. "I guess your pine trees make one hungry."

"Hark!" breathed Laurel. "I heard a step!"

The next moment Cora stood at the entrance to the hut, and waited. The step was coming closer and closer! And it was plainly that of a man!

"Oh, what can it be?" gasped Laurel. "Or who is it?"

"I - I don't know," whispered Cora, her voice trembling in spite of herself. "But we must be brave, Laurel, brave."

"Oh, yes, I will be! Oh I how glad I am that some one is with me - that you are here!"

Cora felt the other's frail body trembling as she put her own strong arms around the shrinking girl. Then Cora peered from the door of the hut. Still that stealthy footstep till the approach of that unknown. Cora felt as if she must scream, yet she held her fears in check - not so much for her own sake as for the other.

Suddenly there was a crash in the underbrush, the crackling of brushes, the breaking of twigs.

"He - he's fallen!" gasped Laurel.

"Tripped over something," added Cora. "Oh, maybe he will turn back now."

Them was silence for a moment and then, to the relief of the girls, they heard footsteps in retreat. Their unwelcome visitor was going away.

"Oh, he's gone! He's gone!" gasped Laurel in delight.

"Maybe it wasn't a man at all," suggested the practical Cora. "It might have been a bear - or - er some animal."

"There are no bears on this island," replied her companion with a wan smile - no animals bigger than coons, and they couldn't make so much a noise. Besides, I heard him grunt, or moan, as he fell. So it must have been a man."

"Well, he's gone," rejoined Cora, "and, now that he's left us alone I'm going to hope that he didn't hurt himself. He interrupted our supper and now it's time we finished it," and in the dim light of the lantern they ate the coarse food and waited - waited for what would happen next.

CHAPTER XVII

THE SEARCHING PARTY

"I know something has happened to Cora," Hazel was lamenting, "and I am afraid we have lost good time in not going with the boys. Let us get ready at once. Here Bess and Belle, you take these lanterns, Nettie carry matches - and take a strong mountain stick, and -"

"Oh, mercy!" exclaimed Belle, in terror, "why should we need a strong stick!"

"To make our way with," replied the practical Hazel. "It is not easy to get about in woods on a dark night like this," and she gave a look at the lights to make sure they were all right. "The boys were to send word here, or to leave word with Ben if they found her. Now let's hurry."

It was a sad little party that started off from Camp Cozy. When, that evening, according to the note Cora had left on the hanging lamp, she did not appear, for some little time, there was scarcely any anxiety. Cora was so reliable, and of course they could conjecture a dozen things that might have detained her. But when an hour passed, and she then was not to be found, Jack jumped up, Ed and Walter followed, and as they hurried off, left the word that through Ben, or by message to camp, they would report to the girls.

Now another whole hour had passed, and there was

no message.

"Which way shall we go - ?" asked tenderhearted Bess.

"To the landing first," Hazel replied. She was always leader in Cora's absence.

This was but a short way from the camp. At the landing stood Ben with his faithful lantern.

"They've got her boat," he blurted out.

"Where?" asked the girls in chorus.

"Just in the cove. But nothin' could hev hurt her there. She ain't drownded in that cove."

"But how could her boat get there?" demanded Hazel.

"No way but to be run in there," answered Ben. "I tell you, girls, this is some trick. 'Taint her fault of course, but she's all right somewhere."

The thought of the man Jones flashed through Hazel's mind. And he had threatened Cora. She had interfered in taking away Kate, the house keeper, she had found out about the man and girl on Fern Island, and she had saved little Mabel Blake! Now all that -

"Trick!" repeated Bess. "That could not be called a trick."

"For want of a better word," said Ben, with apology in his voice. "But when the boys found the boat they started off in her and left word you were not to follow."

"But we must," insisted Hazel. "We might find her and they might not. But how can we go?"

"I could get you another boat if you're set on it," offered Ben, "but I wouldn't like to displease the young men."

"Oh, we will answer for that," Hazel assured him, "just get the boat. We will go up the lake."

"Yes, you've got it right. Up the lake, fer I saw Tony comin' down the lake."

Only Hazel understood him. He, too, suspected the man of many names.

It was not more than five minutes later that Dan brought the small motor boat from the dock, and scarcely more than another five minutes passed before the girls were off.

There were many small boats dotted about the water, and the girls looked keenly for the flag of the Petrel which they could have distinguished even in the darkness for the white head-light always showed up its maroon and white, but old Ben took no heed of the craft in the lower end of the cove. He headed straight for either Far or Fern Island - the twin spots of land far away.

Out in the broadest part of the water they suddenly came upon a rowboat without a light.

"Look out there!" shouted Ben. "Where's your light?"

There was no answer. Ben turned as far out of his course as it was possible to do at the rate his own boat was running.

"There is no one in that boat," declared Hazel. "See, it is just drifting."

"Might be," said Ben, throttling down his gasoline so that he might turn nearer the other craft for inspection.

"There does not seem to, be any one in it," declared Bess, who also looked over the edge of the smaller boat.

Ben did not reply. He had recognized the other craft as that belonging to Jim Peters, and guessed that the man might be up to some trick. When he had almost stopped his motor he jumped up and peered into the rowboat.

"'Low there!" he called "Sleepin -?"

There was no answer.

"Hum," he sniffed, "thought so. It's Jim. Say there Jim, you're not over friendly."

Thus taunted the man in the other boat moved to the low seat. He growled rather than spoke, but Ben was not the sort to take offence at a fellow like Jim.

"Joy riding?" persisted Ben.

"Say, you smart 'un," spoke Peters, "when you want to be funny better try it on some 'un else. Leave me alone," and he picked up the oars and sculled off.

"What do you suppose he was hiding for?" asked Belle.

"Oh he always has somethin' up his sleeve," replied Ben with a light laugh, "and the best we can do is to follow him."

"But then we cannot look farther for Cora," Objected Hazel.

"The best way to find her is to make sure that he does not find her first," said Ben. "She's all right so long as we keep her away from her enemies," and he turned the boat down the lake toward the landing.

Margaret Penrose

CHAPTER XVIII

FOUND

From the finding of Cora's boat to the landing at Fern Island the boys lost little time. Somehow Jack felt the night's work had to do with the hermit and his daughter; also he feared that the man Jones might know of it, so that he lost no time in hurrying to the far end of the lake in hope of there finding his sister.

Few words were spoken by the three boys as they landed, took the lanterns from the motor boat, and after detaching the batteries, to make sure no one would run off with the craft, they sought a path in the wilderness.

Good fortune, or kind fate, led them in the right direction. They could see that the way had been beaten down. They walked on, one ahead of the other, when Jack, who was in the lead, stopped.

"What's this?" he exclaimed, stooping to pick up a white thing from the ground. "A letter," he finished, holding out a square envelope.

The other young men drew nearer to Jack, to examine what might prove to be an unexpected clew.

"What do you make of it?" asked Ed.

"It's - er -" Jack paused suddenly. On the envelope he had caught, in the light of a slanting ray from a lantern a girl's name - "Laurel." He had been on the point of taking the missive from its cover, but the glimpse of that name prevented him. Somehow he felt that it might have to do with the disappearance of Cora - she was always getting mixed up with girls, he reflected. And it might not be just the best thing to publish broadcast what this was Jack dissimulated.

"I guess it's some shooting license a hunter has dropped," he completed his half-finished sentence. "I'll just stick it in my pocket until we get to a place where I can look at it better. I might lose something from the envelope in the woods. Come on, boys."

"I think we're on the right trail," spoke Walter.

"But where in the world can Cora be?" asked Jack. He was beginning to be very much disturbed and was under a great mental strain.

"Let's yell!" suggested Ed. "If Cora is within hearing distance she'll hear us."

"Good!" cried Jack. "All together now!"

They raised their voices in a shrill cry that carried far.

As the echoes died away there seemed to come, from a distance, an echo of an echo. They all started as they heard it.

"Hark!" commanded Jack, standing at attention.

"It's a voice all right - an answer," declared Walter.

"Yes," agreed Cora's brother. "It was over this way. Come on, boys!"

Together they dashed through the bushes, trampling the

underbrush beneath their feet. The lanterns they carried gave but poor light and more than once they crashed into trees. But they kept on, stopping now and then to call again and listen for the answer.

"Look! A light!" suddenly cried Jack, pointing off to the left.

"Come on!" shouted Ed, and they changed their course. Five minutes more of difficult going, for they had gotten off the path, brought them to the pine hut. In the doorway stood two girls with their arms about each other.

"Cora!" gasped Walter and Ed in one voice. "And the other may be - Laurel," murmured Jack, and then he too cried: "Cora!"

The next instant he had his sister in his arms, and there arose a confused clamor of joyful voices, each person trying to talk above the others.

"And - and you are really alive!" cried Jack, holding his sister off at arm's length and gazing fondly at her.

"Yes, Jack," was the glad response. "You see, Jack dear, it takes a good deal to do away with me."

"But - but something surely happened!" he insisted.

"Of course it did, but I'm not going to tell you about it now."

"Yes, make her, Jack!" insisted Walter and Ed.

"And your friend," added Cora's brother in a low voice.

"Oh, I almost forgot," she replied. "Boys, this is Laurel - Wild Laurel if you like. Laurel, these are the boys, including my brother. You can easily tell who he is," she added dryly. "More formal introductions can wait."

"Tell us what happened," demanded Jack, and then Cora briefly related what had taken place since she came to the island, how she had discovered the loss of her boat and had found Laurel and the old hermit. She told of their parting from Laurel's father and how she and her companion had returned to the hut.

"And then - then some one came toward the hut after we got here," she finished. "And, oh, how frightened we were! But whoever it was went away again and didn't bother us. Then we ate something and - and well, you know the rest."

"It's all right," Ed soothed, realizing that both girls had been terribly frightened. "We just came from the lake by your path. It's splendid to find you Cora," and he went over to press her hand. "And I am sure you and your friend are glad to be found."

Cora looked up, and in the dim lantern light she could be seen to smile. "It was all because someone took my boat," she said in a braver voice. "Laurel and I were just going to the main land."

"As soon as you feel able we will take you to the boat," suggested Jack. "It must have been very bad here for you, and with some one else loose in the woods."

"Oh, it was," said Cora. "Jack, I have been in many dreadful places, but on an island with an enemy prowling about seems to be the most fearful."

"An enemy?" repeated Walter.

"Yes, that man Tony, or Jones, took my boat," declared Cora, indignantly, "and this time I will not try to make the laws myself. I am sure he took your canoe, and now my boat!"

"Well, we have you anyway," said Jack giving his sister a great warm embrace, "and now we are going to take you both back to civilization. Walter, can you care for Miss Laurel?"

And then Jack, seeing a good chance, slipped into Laurel's hand the envelope he had picked up in the woods. The girl started, stared at him for a moment, and then hid the missive from sight. She did not speak, but looked her thanks to Jack.

So happy were the girls to get away and to be in such safe company, that the shock and exhaustion following it were almost forgotten. Cora felt much stronger, and so did Laurel. They looked like two very much tossed and tousled girls, but the boys were not thinking of their looks just then.

"Are we going in my own boat?" asked Cora, showing how the ownership of that boat had been so dear to her.

"In the Pet!" replied Ed, "Jack, let me help Cora; you take the light."

Walter, waited for Laurel. She seemed to have things to take with her from the hut. "A queer camp, isn't it?" she asked, "but it's a great little place on a warm clay."

"Or a dark night," dared Walter, whereat Ed threatened to take both girls and so leave the wily Walter alone - for punishment.

The girls laughed. "Walter is our champion," explained Cora. "I shouldn't wonder if it were he who found us."

"Never," contradicted Jack. "I - found you."

"That's a good, dear, old Jackie," replied Cora assuming something of her old-time lightheartedness. "Of course, Jack, you knew!"

Laurel was fumbling in her blouse. The others noticed the movement. "Just a picture I want to take," she explained. "You see, this is quite an old camp."

They saw but they did not understand. Then they started out in the darkness.

"Did you ever see such a black night?" asked Cora, "I had no idea Cedar lake was so - so threatening!"

"Never!" replied Ed.

"But the water is just as friendly as ever," declared Jack. "Now let us try it." He untied the boat, and the party stepped in. Cora pressed Laurel's hand in silent encouragement for she saw her turning her eyes toward Fern Island.

"A lovely boat," Laurel remarked too quietly for the young men to hear her.

"Shall I speed her?" asked Jack opening the gas valve.

"Oh, yes, let us get home," begged Cora. "The girls must be frightened to death."

"They are," Walter assured her. "Belle was smelling kerosene to keep up, when we left," he went on superciliously.

"And Hazel was looking for a club," Jack announced.

"What about Bess, Ed?" asked Cora.

"Bess - oh Bess, she was puffing - for breath. Bess had the puffs," he volunteered in a weak attempt at nonsense.

They were running down the lake. It seemed as if the boat knew exactly where to go, and also that her own mistress was aboard.

"Why, there's the landing!" exclaimed Cora, "how quickly we got here."

"And there is a crowd around. I'll wager they are there to

welcome us," said Jack happily.

For a few moments all waited to see how the crowd would take the news of the finding of Cora.

"There are a lot of lights," remarked Ed in puzzled tones.

"And boats," added Walter.

They were looking intently at the center of the crowd on the water.

"What's going on over there?" asked Jack, looking up from the engine which he was slowing down.

"Something must have happened," answered Cora. "Hark! There's a lot of excited talk."

Across the water floated the murmur of voices, some of them raised high in discussion.

"What's going on?" called Jack to a man who slipped past the side of the Petrel in a rowboat.

"Fight!" was the quick answer. "Jim Peters and a fellow they call Tony. They had a quarrel about some papers and a girl, and I don't know what not."

"A girl?" gasped Cora, wondering if she could be involved in the unpleasantness.

"Well, that's what some say. I don't rightly know. Guess it didn't amount to much. Anyhow they've got Peters over there in his boat. They're bringing him to a doctor. It seems Tony whacked him with a boat hook, and then, thinking he'd done serious damage, he leaped overboard and swam for it. They can't find him."

"And I don't believe they ever will," put in another voice, and as a second boat came up Cora recognized old Ben. "Ah, it's Miss Kimball and her friends," he added as he saw Cora and those in the Petrel. "Now here's a chance for you to use your brains, Miss Cora. Can't you find Tony for us?"

"No, why should I," she answered somewhat coolly.

She did not quite like this familiarity.

"Oh, I didn't know," laughed Ben genially. "I just thought you always like to be doing things."

"Not that kind," put in Jack.

"Is Peters much hurt?" asked Ed.

"It's hard to say," answered Ben. "He's pretty tough and I guess it's hard to do him much damage. I'm going over to see about it."

He rowed over toward where the other boats were congregated and the Petrel with the slow progress of which he had been keeping pace, swung on to the dock. Cora and the others could see the return of the little flotilla about the boat in which was Jim Peters.

CHAPTER XIX

IN BRIGHTER MOOD

It takes but a small happening to furnish excitement for a small place, and the fact that Jim and Tony had quarreled, and that near the landing, created quite a buzz. Of course, much disliked as Jim was, he was one of the regular fishermen, while Tony was a comparative stranger. This caused the latter to disappear when he saw that he had knocked Jim down and had perhaps seriously injured him.

The landing of Cora and the meeting with her friends was almost unnoticed. It was the fight, and the possible hope of more of it, that occupied the morbid crowd.

"Cora! Cora!" the girls were exclaiming, each evidently trying to be the most exclamatory.

"Where have you been?" asked the ever-wise Hazel.

"Why, just getting Laurel," replied Cora as Belle loosed her hold on Cora's neck. "Belle dear, be careful," she begged, "my neck is awfully sunburned."

"We were scared to death," declared Bess, fanning herself with her handkerchief. "We thought you had been kidnapped."

"No, it was the boat that was kidnapped," replied Cora, "A boat is more useful than - "

"Now, Cora," interrupted Ed, "just be careful. Didn't we go after you? And didn't we carry you off?"

Laurel had taken Jack's advice and was resting on an old beam that lay alongside the dock. She was very pale, as one could see even in the uncertain light. Yet her sudden restoration to something like strength might be accounted for by the fact that she had eaten some food in the hut, the previous fast having weakened her greatly. Or was it the letter Jack gave her?

"It's wonderful to be back again," remarked Cora. "You have no idea how far away Fern Island is at night."

"Oh, dreadful!" exclaimed Belle. "I would have died."

"Poor place for dying," put in Ed. "'Twould be like the babes in the wood, and the birdies and the leaves and all that sort of thing. Even to die, Belle, one may do it up in style."

"I don't think you should make a joke of death," objected Belle, pouting.

"Oh, I didn't," declared Ed. "I was only trying to make a joke out of the idea of you being able to die - any place. You never will, Belle. You will go on being nice forever, like the brook."

The crowd had now scattered, so that the girls might make their way along to camp without brushing through the throng. They had left their boat at the landing, in order to see the girls, who, Jack declared, were waiting there. They could now go aboard again and finish the journey.

"Say folks," said Ed in a merry voice, "I propose that we make for the camp. We are starved, every one of us.

"And Laurel must be actually weak," added Cora, "for all sorts of adventures interfered with our supper."

Seeing the canoe girl, the others drew up to her. Whispered

remarks were politely passed, but Jack kept winking and making queer signs toward Walter. Cora joined in the mirth as well as she could but was still nervous. As Cora's boat was setting out, Ben leaned over and whispered:

"Don't listen to word from any one, and what's more, if you know anything about the cause for this fight keep it close-to yourself. I told your brother the rest," and he covered her small white hand with his own brown rough palm.

"Thank you, Ben, and yes, I will remember," said Cora, with more stress in her voice than in her words. Then the Petrel puffed up to Camp Cozy.

There all attention was bestowed upon Laurel. The girl had gone from shock to shock until she was really in need of rest and nourishment. Of course Cora made light of her own predicament. She admitted she had been frightened when she found the boat gone, and Laurel sick, but tried to laugh and call it just one more experience, that would add to her general knowledge. But her face was white, and even Belle and Bess who had risen from prostration to over-joy could not be deceived.

"It's about that man Peters," Bess whispered to Belle. "You know she had some interest in him because she felt he knew about the hermit and the girl. But the girl is here now," she finished, unable further to explain Cora's agitation.

It was Jack who made the opportunity for Cora to talk privately with him, and the sister was not averse to seizing it.

Jack called her to the side porch directly after she had had some refreshments.

"What's worrying you, sis?" he asked kindly, putting his arm around her.

"Oh, Jack, I don't know. If you hadn't come!" and she

shivered as she thought of that dire possibility.

"Oh, but we did come. We found you much sooner than we thought we would, and I must say you weren't half so frightened as you had a right to be under the circumstances. You are one of the bravest girls I ever saw - that's right and so is that Wild Laurel."

"Oh, I just love her Jack," said Cora warmly, "and if only this other thing about her father comes right, I shall not in the least regret the experience that brought us together. It is a great story, Jack. You know we have still to rescue her father."

"The hermit?" he asked.

"Yes, an outcast, for some mysterious reason. But we shall soon clear that up when Laurel is strong enough to be questioned. I feel so much better," and she kissed him as if he and she were just the babies they felt themselves to be on such occasions.

"Jack," she whispered, a little later, "I am just going to think it is all right. You can count on me. I am not going to have nervous prostration from so small a thing as to-night's happenings."

"Good, sis," and his second kiss was applause for her own. "Of course, you are the brickiest kind of brick. And so is Laurel, a Russet brick. Isn't she that?"

"Exactly that," and Cora started toward the room. "She will be a perfectly dear girl when she gets back to civilized ways. Hush, here she comes?"

"Cora," breathed Laurel, who now had on a robe that Belle insisted had been made for her, though her own mother had ordered it for Belle, "Cora, who was the man in the boat that was hurt?"

Wondering how the girl could have escaped overhearing the

name Peters, Cora replied:

"A fisherman I believe, but he may not have been much hurt. Folks in such places as these cling to every sensation, and fix it up to suit themselves."

"But how will they find his assailant?" asked the girl, interested for some unknown reason.

Cora glanced at Jack. "They will look for him of course," Jack replied for his sister.

"Where was he hurt?" Laurel persisted.

"We have no reason to think he was hurt at all," said Jack decidedly. "It's only rumor, and if you don't mind my dictation, I should suggest that this be a forbidden subject. It is about the worst thing either of you can think of."

"Right brother, always right!" said Cora. "Now let us go in and try to make the girls happy with a little part of our story. You can trust me, Laurel," she said aside. "I know just what they want to know."

"Oh," breathed Bess, as Cora and Laurel entered the pretty, bright, little sitting room, "is it possible that our troubles are over for one night?"

"No, I see more kinds of trouble ahead," and of course she looked at the irresistible and irrisisting Walter. "Don't they match?" aside to Belle, whose ideas of color schemes and whose regard for the beautiful were blamed for the inflection of nerves.

"They do," she agreed. "Her hair is just russet-brown, and her eyes hazel. Oh, I have always loved that sort of face when it goes with the olive skin."

"How did you know that I had named her Russet?" asked Jack,

touching with mock concern one stray yellow curl that threatened Belle's sight.

"I did not," she replied, "but I think it suits her exactly. And Walter is all of a shade."

"Oh, Belle. I am going to tell him? Wallie shady!"

"You know perfectly well, Jack Kimball, I said shade - in color."

"Oh, yes. Color blind. Poor, afflicted Wallie. I have often wondered about his neckties. But doesn't Laurel take to him? And isn't she a beaut in that bag?"

"Bag! My best kimono! Look what teeth she has when she laughs."

"And you not jealous? Belle I think, after all, I shall have to return to my first love," and he slipped his arm all the way back of her steamer chair, for Jack dearly loved to tease either Bess or Belle, declaring what happened to one twin would react on the other.

"Hazel cannot take her eyes off of Cora. I might be jealous there," reported the blonde twin.

"You may 'jell' all you like on that score," Jack consented. "But hello! Here's Paul!"

The tall, dark boy, Paul Hastings, Hazel's brother, had just entered the door. Instantly he was overcome with the welcome, for while the boys fell to kissing him and smoothing his hair in the most approved lover-like way, the girls crowded around and offered him empty plates and glasses of flowers, to say nothing of Bess, with the Japanese parasol, who stood over his chair while Cora fanned him.

Laurel looked on like one who enjoys a play. There seemed in her eyes something to indicate that such a scene was not entirely new to her, but was for some time forgotten. Presently Cora remembered that Laurel had not met Paul before, and so introduced them. She merely said Laurel in mentioning names, but the omission of anything so unimportant as a last title would never be noticed among these young folks.

"Say now, let a fellow breathe" begged Paul, "and also let him puff out a little. There! I feel better! And I just want to remark that I have found the lost canoe!"

At the words "lost canoe" Laurel started. Cora saw her, and slipped over to her side.

"You need not worry, dear. Everything is safe with us," whispered Cora, pressing the other's hand.

"Our old original! You don't mean it?" exclaimed Ed.

"None other," declared Paul. "And I wonder you did not find it before."

"Where was it?" asked Walter.

"Tied up to your own dock. I just spied it as I landed."

"Oh, you go on," threatened Jack. "Do you think we are teething?"

"No, jollying," vowed Paul. "I just this minute guessed it."

Without more comment the entire party hurried out the door, and made for the dock. Jack won first place and so held the lantern.

"She's red," he declared. "While ours was green."

"Just a matter of time," said Paul in his delightfully easy way. "Most girls are green when they come up here, and -"

Ed's hand was over Paul's mouth so he could not complete the joke. Jack was looking for the tell-tale piece of wood that had been inserted in the end of the canoe to mend a slight break.

"Yep, sure it's her," he declared.

"SHE!"' yelled the girls. "Jack!" Cora's voice came, "how can you so shock our English?"

"Pardon me, ladies," he murmured. "But this is it."

"Painted red," Belle was trying to realize out loud.

"Yes, and it's right becoming," agreed Ed, "but where did she get the sun-burn?"

"The Mystery of her Complexion, or, the Shade of Her Pretty Nose," quoth Jack. "Well, I don't mind. But I would like to get hold of The Silent Artist of Cedar Lake," he finished, in crude eloquence.

Paul was looking carefully inside the canoe. Presently he stood up straight, and held a note in his hand. "Let's have the light Jack?" he asked. "I have something."

Jack held the lantern so that it's gleam fell on the paper. "Miss Cora Kimball," they both read, then they handed the paper to Cora.

It was enclosed in an envelope of very fine linen; Cora saw this instantly, for she felt, as well as saw, the texture. Just as she was about to tear open the missive a thought occurred to her.

"I had best wait until I get indoors," she said. "I might drop something out of it here and break the charm."

A murmur of disapproval followed this remark. But Cora won out, and with much apprehension carried the strange letter inside. Under the light she looked first at the signature. It was Brentano!

CHAPTER XX

LAUREL'S FLIGHT

"What is it? What is it?" demanded the girls in chorus.

Cora made light of her actions as she hid the note, but in reality she had no idea of reading it before any one. What might it not contain?

"I get so few love letters," she remarked, "that I want a chance to enjoy them."

"Then as that's the case," said Ed, "it's us for the Bungle. Come on, boys," and he pretended offence, "Us is hurt."

"Now Ed, I said letters - not lovers," corrected Cora.

"The pen and ink!" demanded Ed. "I will to thee a letter indite," and he opened the small desk in the darkest corner of the room.

This was a signal for every boy to pretend to write a love letter to every girl. Jack could get nothing better than a feather from the Indian headpiece that hung on the wall. This he dipped in Belle's shoe dressing, and wrote a note on the back of Cora's best piece of sheet music. Walter sat on the floor poking his whittled stick into the dead embers in the fire-place, and managed to scratch something on a fan - it belonged to Bess. Paul did not much care for nonsense, but appropriately made

Margaret Penrose

Indian characters on the wooden bowl with his pen knife. The whole turned out more fun than was expected.

Walter proffered his love letter to Laurel, and she surprised them all by reading this:

"My Mountain Laurel:

Meet me when the buds come and we will wait for the blossoms.

Your Bending Bough."

The cue that Laurel furnished was taken up by the others and when Jack offered his "note" to Hazel she read.

"My Dear Burr:

Be patient and you will loose the green, Hazelnuts are never soft!

Yours,

The Fellow Who Fell Down Hill with Jill."

Cora read what Ed did not write:

"My Reef:

When stranded I know what to grab - Your larder is ever my rock of refuge.

Yours, Co-Ed."

Belle and Bess both partook of Paul's note, and as Paul was acknowledged the artist of them all the double missive was gladly accepted by the twins - as doubles.

Belle pretended to read:

"Two to one, or two in one,

Double the wish and double the fun."

The merry making that followed this little farce was of too varied a character to describe. Some of the boys insisted on standing on their heads while others took up a low mournful dirge that might have done credit to the days of the red men and wigwams.

Finally, Cora insisted that it was late - disgracefully late - for campers to have lights burning, and the boys were obliged to leave for their own quarters. Going out, Jack whispered to Cora:

"Ben told Paul to say to you that under no circumstances were you to go down to the landing to-morrow. I know he has some good reason for the warning. The row between Peters and Brentano may not have ended there," and he kissed her good night. "We have had a jolly time and to-morrow when I come you must let me see the mysterious love letter."

Cora promised, and then the lights were turned out.

Making sure that all, even Laurel, were sleeping Cora slipped out into the sitting room, relighted the lamp and unfolded the note that had been found in the canoe.

She felt her heart quicken. Why did she fear and yet long to know what that man had to tell her? She read:

"YOUNG LADY:

When you receive this I shall be too far away to further meet your daring, baffling challenge of my plans. What I intend to do I can not even tell myself, for everything seemed so easy of evil until you crossed my path. So easy was it that there was even no victory in the spoils. But first you came boldly to the den of poor Peters. Then you deliberately took from us that simple-minded, harmless old woman, Kate; next you did not call out when she gave you back your ring - not call out against us. All this to me was incomprehensible. Why should a young girl not fear us? Why should she not denounce us? Then you saved that little doll, Mabel Blake, until finally I began to wonder why I, a talented high-born Italian, should pretend to love crime when a mere girl could be a noble defender?

The difference made me feel like a coward, and I decided finally to go away. Before I left I had trouble with Peters. This hurried me and I have not time to write more now. I know you got back from the island - boys of your kin do not wait long to find their sisters. By to-morrow noon, if all goes well with me on the journey, I shall be able to write that to poor little Laurel which will release her from her bondage. I will send the letter care of you. Thank the boys for use of their canoe.

BRENTANO."

For some moments Cora sat looking blankly at that fine foreign paper. What a splendid hand! What direct diction!

And her conduct had influenced him to turn away from his evil ways. She had done nothing more than others, except perhaps she had more courage, born of better and more complete experience. She sighed a sigh of satisfaction as she again hid the paper in her gown. Then with one great heart-beat of prayerful thanksgiving, she, too, sought "tired nature's sweet restorer."

It was the sound of dishes and the tinkle of pans that awoke Cora next morning. Day so soon! And all the others up!

"Now, we have fooled you," said Belle with a light laugh. "You have slept longest!"

Cora had been dreaming very heavily, and her sleep seemed but a reflection of the previous day's troubles. Now she was awake and instantly she remembered it all about Ben telling her not to go near the landing; then about the letter.

"Is Laurel up?" she asked.

"No, we let her sleep to keep you company," said Hazel, "and we are going to give you such a surprise for breakfast! Don't tell, girls."

Cora slipped into a robe and stepped across the room to peer into the little corner where Laurel had gone to her rest.

"Laurel is up," she declared. "She is not here!"

"Not there! Not in bed! Laurel - she has not gotten up yet," declared Belle, who with frying pan in hand had hurried from the kitchen when Cora spoke.

"She certainly is not in bed," again declared Cora. "You may see for yourselves."

"Laurel gone!" exclaimed more than one of the astonished girls.

"She may have gone out," suggested Hazel. "I thought I heard someone about very early."

Following this thought the girls looked around called, and again returned to the empty room.

"What is this?" asked Bess, seeing a piece of ribbon-tied paper floating from the night lamp.

Hazel was first to handle it. She saw that it was a note addressed to Cora.

"It's for you, Cora," she said as she snapped the fragile ribbon from its fastening.

Cora read aloud:

"Forgive me for going this way but I could not wait longer to know about my father. I will return before dark and bring with me the canoe I have borrowed. You may, trust me and need not be anxious.

Gratefully,

LAUREL STARR."

"Gone in the canoe!"

"I know why, girls," Cora admitted, "and if you will all come in here together I will tell you as much, as I myself know. The real story I have not yet been able to learn, but must do so very soon."

Then she told of the first discovery of the man on Fern Island, following with the account of her second and third visits there, and finally of how she found poor Laurel in such distress the night of her own exile. The loss of her boat they all knew about, and that part was a certain kind of clear mystery.

"Laurel has gone back to see about her father," she finished. "It is only natural, and I should have thought it strange had she not done so."

"Of course," added Bess, brushing away a tear. "Poor little wild Laurel had to go back, it was almost as cruel to keep her as to pen up a brown bunny."

In spite of the seriousness of the moment every one smiled. First Laurel was russet, now compared to a little brown rabbit.

"We had just gotten acquainted with her," murmured Belle. "I thought her so romantic."

"And I thought her so intelligent," put in the ever-studious

Hazel. "Even Paul took the trouble to notice her."

"Well, we will have her back again," promised Cora. "I am positive she will keep her word. I think her a splendid girl. All she needs is the chance to get over the state of chronic fright she has been living in. Then she will be just as normal as any of us."

"Then, that being the case," said Hazel, with a jump, "I propose we keep normal by eating our breakfast. I am famished, and those boys almost emptied the ice-box."

"Nettie had to go away into town for eggs," Bess orated, "and therefore we had to do all the cooking."

"It smells all right," Cora said, as they pulled the chairs to the table. "Let us hope we will get through one meal without interruption. My appetite is positively canned."

"And I took the trouble to gather those morning glories," Belle announced. "I thought Laurel would like them."

"They are beautiful, Belle," said Cora, looking with admiration at the dainty green vines with their freshly-blown, colored bells that trailed from the glass bowl in the center of the table. "Nothing could be more artistic, and we enjoy them even if Laurel has missed them," Cora finished.

"But the food," demanded Hazel. "It is of that we sing. Food, food! Isn't it good; a girl is a loon who can't eat what she could," sang Hazel, with more mirth than English.

"Eggs, eggs, bacon and eggs."

"She eats all she can, then sits up and begs," sang Cora helping herself to that portion of the fare, and keeping time with the humming toast.

Bess was taking her third slice of bread. That inspired Belle.

"Bread, bread, Nettie's good bread -"

"When Bess took the loaf, we nearly fell dead," sang out Belle, rescuing the much-worn loaf from which Bess was trying to get a slice.

"The toasts are very well as far as they go," commented Cora, "but I notice that the food stuffs go farther."

"And the boys are coming at ten," remarked Hazel. "I'm glad I cooked. I don't have to wash the dishes."

"But the boys were going out in the canoe and now it's gone," Belle reminded them. "They were going to take the prize canoe, and the red one, and we would all then have a chance to float out together. Now, of course, we won't be able to go."

"We can go in our own boat," Cora said, "and really the lake is quite rough for canoeing this morning. When Laurel comes back she will likely bring her own boat and then we will have three in our fleet."

"Why couldn't you, and she come home in her canoe when you found your boat gone, Cora?" asked Bess suddenly.

"Hers was not at the dock - someone had borrowed it," Cora explained without explaining.

They had about finished their meal. Belle was already snatching the dishes, in spite of protests that there was some perfectly good eating which had not yet been eaten.

"There come the boys now," announced Hazel. "They look sort of-gloomy."

Cora glanced out of the window and saw Ed, Jack and Walter strolling along the path. She, too, thought they looked "gloomy," but it was not her practice to anticipate trouble.

The "hellos" were exchanged before the young men had time to enter the camp. Then Belle asked:

"Aren't we going canoeing?"

"Guess not to-day," replied Ed, his handsome black hair almost sparkling in the sunshine as he tossed his head in nonchalance. "We are still too cramped up. Had to sleep on the roof last night."

"Why?" demanded Cora.

"Choosin' that. My little joke," he replied, "Girls, I'm cuttin' up," and he tried to hide a serious air with a ridiculous remark. "But we'll do something. We'll go fishin'" he declared.

"We thought it best to keep out in the cove this morning," Jack was explaining to Cora. "There is so much going on around the landing."

"What is going on?" she asked rather nervously.

"Oh, that Peter's affair," replied her brother with assumed indifference. "They are looking him over to-day to see how much he's hurt."

"Oh!" said Cora vaguely. Then she went indoors from the porch to prepare for the fishing trip.

CHAPTER XXI

MOTOR TROUBLES

"It is strange Laurel does not come back," remarked Bess, as the girls sat on the porch after a most unsuccessful fishing trip (as far as fish were concerned), "Somehow I feel she would if she could."

"That's it exactly," Cora corroborated. "If she could get back here this afternoon, we would have seen her. But then her father may have been too lonely without her, or any of many other things may have detained her."

Cora jumped up suddenly, and skipped down the path to where her motor boat was fastened. She would look over the engine. The wire connections had slipped, and she would tighten them, and make some other minor adjustments.

Cora found more to do on her boat than she had expected. The boys had had the craft out latest and had neglected to put down the oil cup levers. This caused the cylinder to be flooded with lubricant, and if there was one thing Cora disliked more than another it was to run an oil puffing boat, and "inhale the fumes."

She pulled on her heavy gloves and got to work to drain out the oil through the base cock. Bending over her task she did not see, neither did she hear, an approaching person. It was Ben.

"Busy, eh?" he said in his splendid, candid way. Cora was so glad it was only Ben.

"Oh yes," she replied, "the boys never seem to know how to leave a boat. This is thoroughly oil-soaked."

"They're careless that way," admitted Ben, stepping into the boat to see what the trouble was. "If I were you I would make some rules and tack 'em down by the license card."

"They would never read them," Cora declared. "There - just look at that oil," as she collected some in a funnel. "This would have made the muffler smoke like a locomotive."

Ben looked at the oil cups. "There isn't any thing meaner than running a boat that throws out soft coal smoke," he admitted. "Those boys left the plungers up. But I say, girl, where's your new friend?"

"Laurel?" asked Cora as she put the wrench in the tool box.

"Yes. I thought she had come down here to stay."

"Well, we thought so too, but then she could not be expected to leave the island - all at once," and Cora wondered if she were saying too much.

"It's queer to me," went on Ben. "Them fellows have something to do with that," and he nodded his head toward the landing.

"You mean - Peters and Tony?"

"Yes. And what I want to say, Miss, is this. You had best keep clear of them. The row at the landing isn't exactly fixed up. I think it had to do with something at Fern Island."

"About Laurel?"

"Yes. I have suspected for a long time that the little runs that Peters makes up there must have paid him pretty well. Now that he has fallen out with Tony, likely it'll all come to Jim. Best thing we can do, miss, is to keep a sharp look out for the girl. If you can get her to come to camp with you I fancy all the rest will soon straighten itself."

Cora wondered just how much Ben knew of the mystery of that island. She felt obliged to withhold Laurel's secret, yet she felt, too, that Ben would do everything to help her get the girl and the hermit away from their place of exile.

"I'll tell you, Ben," she said finally. "I'll come to you for advice just as soon as I find it is time to act. Depend upon it we are not going to leave Cedar Lake until the mystery of Fern Island is cleared up."

This seemed to satisfy Ben, for beneath the deep brown of his cheeks there showed the glow of color that came with pleasure.

"All right, little girl," he said, "if you want me before I come again, just let me know. Ben will be only too glad to stick by you and all the rest of them," meaning the campers at Camp Cozy and those who bungalowed at the Bungle.

He went off, shambling along with his face turned toward the sky and his feet taking care of themselves. Cora looked after him.

"Dear old Ben," Cora mused, "everything seems worth while when it takes 'everything' to make such a friend as you can be." Then she went back to her engine. She must tighten the wires, and leave the craft in readiness for a quick run.

"Oh, Cora!" came the voice of Bess suddenly, "you've missed it. We have had the most glorious time."

Bess approached, her cheeks as red as the sumac she carried, and her eyes as bright as the very ragged sailors that hung rather dangerously from her belt. "Hasn't Laurel come yet?"

"No, not yet," replied Cora, intent upon her task at the wires. "I am afraid she will hardly come to-night."

"Then we have got to go after her," declared Bess. "Jack said so. He said she could not stay alone on that island all night."

"Oh, did he?" Cora replied in an absent-minded way. "I have had such - a time - with this boat," and she pulled on the wires to make them taut, breaking one and necessitating a splice.

"Can't we take the boat to look for Laurel?" persisted Bess, with more concern than she usually showed.

"Why, of course, I suppose so," said Cora. "There, I guess that will do," and she straightened up with a sigh, for the use of the pliers made her hands ache.

"Why, Cora!" exclaimed Bess, "you look actually pale. You must be awfully tired."

"Me pale," and she laughed. "Now, Bess, don't get romantic. Just fancy me being pale!"

"Well, you are, and I insist that you come back to camp at once and get a drink of warm milk. Cora Kimball, you - look - scared!"

"Oh, I am. Think what it would mean if the boys had knocked my engine out. And it did seem for a time that there was no 'if in it." Cora jumped lightly out of the boat and was ready to greet the other girls. Soon a discussion of color and its causes was in progress, Cora maintaining that her cause of anxiety had been that awful engine and its troubles.

Ed, Walter and Jack had joined the others.

"I say," began Ed, "where do we, go to look for the wild Olive or was it the mountain Laurel? Jack is in a fit, and Walter can't be held. What do you say if we all start out in a searching party? No one has been lost for twenty-four hours, and this state of affairs is getting monotonous."

Without waiting for an answer the girls and boys clambered into the Petrel while Bess went to the camp with Cora who insisted upon washing her hands before making the trip.

"Did anything happen, Cora, while we were away?" asked Bess kindly.

"Not a thing, Bess. I only wish something real would happen; we have so many imitations of excitement."

CHAPTER XXII

THE LAW AND THE LIGHTS

"I want to find her this time," insisted Jack. "Cora, please let me? I promise not to frighten her, and not even to speak to her if you object, but I do so want to find her."

"Seems to me you found her last time," objected Walter who was looking particularly well to-night, for his suit of Khaki and his brown skin seemed all of a piece. "You nearly knocked me down in your haste to find the hut first."

"But," Cora said seriously, "Laurel may not want you boys to find her. She may not even want me to do so. I am just taking chances. Suppose you allow Bess and me or Hazel or any two of us to go up to the hut first? Please do be reasonable, and not silly," Cora finished in a voice she seldom assumed.

"You may come along as dose as you like, until we are just up to the hut," Bess consented, with marked good sense, "as the woods are so thick and black, but when we get to the hut -"

"We can 'hut' it I suppose," snapped Jack. "All right, girls; all I can say is I hope a couple of Brownies, or a mountain lion pay their respects to you both for being so daring."

The boat was running beautifully. The cleaning out that Cora gave the base, and the regulating of the oil cups together with adjusting the wires, helped to make the mechanism run more smoothly, and she glided along without "missing," which means, of course that every explosion was in perfect rhythm to every other explosion. There was a "hot fat" spark as Cora explained.

"There's a big steamer," remarked Hazel, as a large boat glided along.

Cora swung so that the red light of the Petrel showed she was going to the right. The steamer gave two whistles indicating a left course. Cora answered with one blast which meant right. The steamer insisted on left and gave one more signal.

"What's the matter with them?" Jack demanded, taking the steering wheel from Cora. "They seem to own the lake."

No sooner had he said this than the big boat came so close to the smaller craft that a huge wave swept over the small forward deck and instantly the colored lights went out, being drenched. For a moment every one seemed stunned! The shock to the Petrel was as if she had been suddenly dipped into the depths of the lake. But as quickly as it happened just as quickly was it righted, and the offending boat steamed off majestically, as if it had merely bowed to an old acquaintance.

"What do you think of that!" exclaimed Walter, indignantly.

"I think a lot of it," replied Ed, "but the captain of that steamer would not likely want to see my thoughts."

"Small trick," declared Jack, "Even if he had the right to pass us so close, common lake manners obliged him to give in to the smaller boat."

"The lights are both out," Cora said anxiously.

"Well, we are almost to shore," Jack replied, "and it won't be worth while to stop here. We can light up again when we get in."

This seemed reasonable enough and so they sailed along.

"Hello!" exclaimed Walter, "is this another boat trying the same trick?"

A launch was steering very dose to the Petrel. The lights were conspicuously bright, and the engine ran almost noiselessly.

"What is it?" asked Jack, seeing that the captain wanted to speak with some one.

"I want you," replied a voice of authority. "You have no lights."

"Oh, you're the inspector," said Jack candidly. "Well, that steamer that just passed doused our lights, and we are going to land here to relight."

"Sorry, but that's against the law," replied the officer. "You fellows always have an excuse ready, and I can't accept it. You will have to come along with me."

"Arrested!" exclaimed Belle aghast.

"That's about what it amounts to," replied the man coolly. "Can you get in here?"

"Who?" asked Jack.

"The captain," replied the officer grimly.

"Where does he go?" Jack further questioned.

"See here, young man," spoke the inspector rather sharply. "Do you think I've got all night to bother with you?"

"I don't know as I do," replied Jack in the same voice, "but if you will just explain what you want us to do we will give you no further trouble." Jack knew one thing - to refuse to comply with the request of an officer is about the last thing to do if one values either money or liberty.

"That's the way to talk," replied the inspector. "So just suppose you take this rope and I'll tow, you along. I fancy the party would, rather come than let one go alone."

"Of course we would," declared Cora. "In fact I am the captain of this boat."

Jack gave her a meaning bump on the arm - it meant, "let me do the talking," and Cora understood perfectly.

"But where are we going?" wailed Belle, as the man threw the towline to Ed.

"Not far," answered the man. "I just have to take you in, and then you have to do the rest."

"What's the rest?" inquired Walter.

"Oh, pay a fine," said the man carelessly.

"How much?" inquired Ed.

"From five to twenty-five; as the judge sees fit. There, are you fast?"

"Guess so," growled Jack, to whom the arrest seemed like a case of "Captain Kidding."

"And we can't go to Laurel?" Hazel inquired with a sigh.

"Shame," commented Walter under his breath, "but Jack knows the best thing to do with the law is to jolly it."

"Law nothing," muttered Ed, as he took the steering wheel, Jack being busy with the towing line.

"Never mind," Cora suggested. "It will give us a new experience. I had the fool-hardiness to wish for some real excitement this very afternoon."

"But to be arrested!" gasped Bess with a frightened look.

"A distinctly new sensation," said Hazel with an attempt to laugh. "Just think of going before a real, live judge!"

But evidently the other girls did not want to think of it. They would rather have thought of anything else just then.

"Which way are you going?" Jack asked the man in the official boat. "I thought your judge lived on the East side?"

"He does, but we may take some other fellows in yet to-night. This is only one catch," and the inspector laughed unpleasantly.

"They are actually going to tour the lake with us," declared Ed. "If that isn't nerve!"

"Don't complain," cautioned Cora, "perhaps the longer the run the lighter the fine. And we are just waiting for our next allowance."

"And, being a pretty motor-boat, they will make it a pretty fine," mused Walter. "I would like to dip that fellow."

"Yes, they are going to let us tour the lake hitched on to the police boat! The situation is most unpleasant. But there is no way out of it," said Ed, sullenly.

"Suppose they won't take a fine, and want to lock us up?" asked Belle.

"If it were only one night in jail, I'd take it just to fool the man who wants the money, but I am afraid it might be ten days and that would be inconvenient," Jack remarked, as the police boat steamed off with the Petrel trailing. "They call this law. It may be the law but not its intention. We were almost landed, and just about to light up. I tell you they just need the money."

When they reached the bungalow, where judge Brown held his court, the three young men entered with the inspector, and when the judge had satisfied himself that he could not ask more than five dollars and costs for this "first offence" the fine was paid and the matter settled. Belle and Bess were greatly relieved when the culprits came back to the Petrel. They had a hidden fear that something else disgraceful might happen; perhaps the judge would detain the boys, or perhaps the girls would have to go in to testify. Cora's mind was pre-occupied however, and when the Petrel started off, and Jack asked her where to, she said back to Fern Island.

CHAPTER XXIII

A NIGHT ON THE ISLE

It was too late now for Cora to think of making her way to the pine hut without the boys, too dark, too late and too uncertain, so she agreed to allow Ed and Jack to go with her while Walter and the girls followed at some distance.

"There's a light," announced Jack, when they had covered the first hill.

"Yes, that's in the hut," Cora said.

Hurrying before her brother, Cora reached the thatched doorway. She pushed back the screen and saw Laurel leaning over the bed on the floor. As she entered Laurel motioned her not to speak. Then Cora saw that the girl was bending over her father.

"They shall not take me," he murmured. "I am innocent!"

"Hush, father dear," his daughter soothed. "'There is no one here, just your own Laurel," and she bathed his head with her wet handkerchief.

Cora instantly withdrew. She whispered to Jack, and he turned to meet the others, to prevent them coming nearer. Laurel followed her to the open air.

"Father is so changed!" she said under her breath, "while he seems worse, his mind is clearer, and I almost hope he will soon remember everything of the past."

"If his mind is clearer there is every hope for him," Cora replied. "I do hope, Laurel dear, that your exile and his will soon end."

Laurel put her hand to her head as if to check its throbbing. Yes, if it only would soon end!

"What happened?" asked Cora.

"He fell and struck his head on a rock," answered Laurel. "It was that night we were in the hut. It was he who came walking along in the darkness, and we thought it was some one else. He came to look for me after I signaled that time. It was my father!"

"He slipped and fell," she resumed in a moment. "We heard him, you remember, and then - then he went away - my poor father!"

Cora gasped in surprise. "Is he badly hurt?" she managed to ask.

"No, hardly at all. It was only a slight cut on his head, but the shock of it brought him to him self - restored his reason that was tottering. When he got up and staggered off his mind was nearly clear, but he did not dare come to the hut where we were for fear it might contain some of his enemies. He went looking for me, but I had gone with you.

"Since then he has talked of matters he has not mentioned in years and years. But he is not altogether better. Oh, Cora, if his mind would only become strong again, so he could dear up all the mystery!"

'The girls clung lovingly to each other. Then a moan from the hut suddenly called Laurel away, Cora knew Jack was waiting for her in the woods, and she hastened to him.

One whispered sentence to her brother was enough to explain it all to him.

"We must arrange to get him away from here - Laurel's father," he said, as he put his arms about Cora. "Do you think he is strong enough to be moved?"

"I'll ask Laurel," replied Cora joyfully. If only now both the hermit and his daughter could leave that awful island. The other girls stepped to the door in answer to Cora's signal.

"Oh, I am afraid he is too weak for that now," Laurel whispered. "But when he is able I will have him taken to a hospital. That man kept us in terror. Now he is gone and I feel almost free."

"You have heard that he is gone?" questioned Cora.

"I had a letter," replied the other simply, and this answer only served to make a new matter of query for Cora. But she could not ask it now.

"He is sleeping," said Laurel. "Look!"

Cora went over to the pallet and looked down at the man who lay there. Yes, he was noble looking in spite of the growth of his hair and beard, and Cora could see wherein his daughter resembled him. There seemed something like a benediction in that hut, and as the thought stole over her, Cora breathed a prayer that it should not come in the shape of death.

"He's lovely," Cora said to Laurel. "Let us go out and not disturb him."

Jack and the others were waiting silently outside. Cora spoke to her brother. He understood.

Margaret Penrose

"You girls had better go back," he said, "Ed and I will stay here to help Laurel."

"Oh, no, I must stay too. Perhaps in the morning we can take him away," insisted Cora.

Bess and Belle clung together. They had a fear of "the wild man" and it had not yet been dispelled. Hazel tried to induce Laurel to go back to camp and allow her and Cora to care for the father, but of course such an appeal was useless. Laurel would not think of leaving the sick man. It was finally arranged that Cora and Jack should remain, and then reluctantly the others started off with the promise of returning very early the next morning.

"I have some things to eat," Laurel told them. "I thought poor father would like a change, and I got them when I was at the Point."

"Oh, you save them," Jack said. "We had a good supper, and will make out all right until morning. But now tell me where I can get you fresh water."

Cora knew, and she took the extra lantern and started off with her brother. They talked of many things as they stumbled on through the woods.

"There's the spring. Look out! Don't fall in. My isn't that water clear even in the lantern light!" exclaimed Cora suddenly.

Jack filled the pail easily and then they turned back.

"But Jack," Cora began again, "you know there is some mystery about Mr. Starr. That must be his name, for Laurel signed hers so in the note she left."

"Whatever the mystery is, I feet certain it is nothing disgraceful," Jack assured her. "Very likely it was some plot to injure them, concocted by that fellow Jones."

The unfailing reason of this astonished Cora. How could Jack have guessed so near the facts?

"At any rate I think the poor man will be able to be moved in the morning," she finished, as they made their way up the hill. "It will be a wonderful thing if, after all, it comes out all right; that he is a free man, and that his slight injury may restore his scattered faculties."

"Let us hope so," said Jack fervently.

Cora wanted to tell him about the letter from Jones otherwise Brentano, but there was not time to do so before they reached the hut, so she reasoned it would be best to postpone it.

Laurel was sitting, holding her father's injured head when they entered the hut. He was awake now, and looking with such great, hungry eyes into his daughter's face.

"Now we have fresh water, father," she said. "Do you know my friends?"

"The girl, yes," he said 'feebly. "But the boy?"

"Her brother," said Laurel quickly, delight showing in her voice. "Isn't it good to have friends, father?"

"Good, very good," he said. Then he dosed his eyes again, and neither Cora nor Jack ventured to speak.

"It does not seem possible that he can talk so rationally," Laurel whispered. "Oh, I have now such hopes that he will get well."

"Of course he will," Jack assured her. "But you girls had better get some rest. I will sit up and watch."

Cora added her entreaties to those of her brother, and Laurel finally agreed to throw herself down on the straw bed in the far corner of the hut. Cora found room at the other end of the same bed, and presently their young natures gave in to the urgent demands of rest. Jack sat alone watching the white faced man who tossed and turned, muttering incoherent words.

"I did not do it," he would say. "I never saw the note."

"There, you want a drink," said Jack kindly, pressing the tin cup to the trembling lips.

"But Breslin knows! Oh, if I could only find Breslin!"

"Breslin," Jack repeated, astonished.

"Yes, Brendon Breslin. He knows!"

"Brendon Breslin!" Jack said again. This was the name of the wealthy man for whom Paul Hastings ran the fast steam launch.

"Oh, my head!" moaned the man, closing his eyes in pain.

Jack realized that this remark about the millionaire might mean a sudden return of memory, and he resolved to test it further, even at the risk of giving the aching head more pain. For if the memory lapsed again it might never be awakened.

"What does Breslin know?" he asked, leaning very dose to the sick man.

To his surprise the hermit sat bolt upright. "He knows that I never forged the note. It was that sneaking office boy."

That was the story! This man had been made to believe he had forged a note. His exile on the island was because of the supposed crime!

"Of course he knows," Jack soothed. "And to-morrow he will come to see you."

But the sick man was either unconscious, or sleeping. He did not reply.

CHAPTER XXIV

THE UNEXPECTED

"I heard a boat," Cora whispered to Jack, as on the following morning, he rubbed his eyes endeavoring to put sight into them.

"Well, what of it?" he asked.

"It seemed to stop at this landing," replied the sister.

"The girls most likely," and he got to his feet. "How is the old gentleman?"

"Much stronger, and his mind, Laurel thinks, is clearing."

"I think so too. It is an outrage that he has been allowed to suffer here without help. That scoundrel Jones must have fixed this up."

"Did you sleep any, Jack dear?" Cora asked. "I'm afraid you had a lonely vigil."

"Oh, I got a wink or two, and my patient was no trouble. Is that Laurel talking to him?"

"Yes, she seems overjoyed that he can talk rationally to her. But listen Jack! There are voices."

Brother and sister hurried to the door. Strangers were approaching - two men.

"Is - er - Miss Cora Kimball here?" asked one of them, in rather a hesitating voice.

"Yes, what is it?" asked Jack, suspiciously for somehow he did not like the appearance of the strangers.

"We'll do business with her," put in the taller of the two men.

Cora gave a gasp. Somehow she felt as if something unpleasant was about to happen.

"No, you won't do any business with her!" exclaimed Jack, "that is, not until you tell me first. What is it? Out with it!"

"Say, you're quite high and mighty for a young fellow," sneered the short man. "Who be you, anyhow, a lawyer? Because if you are you ought to have sense enough to know that we're detectives, after information, and if we can't get it peaceable we'll get it otherwise. How about that?"

"It doesn't worry me a particle," declared Jack easily. "Now, Cora, leave this to me," for he saw that his sister was much affected. "I'm her brother," he went on, turning to the men, "and not a lawyer, but I guess I can do just as well in this case. Now, what do you want?"

"Well, it's this way," began the tall one. "We heard that Miss Kimball might know something about the quarrel between Peters and Tony, or whatever his name was, and she might be able to put us on his track. Peters is hurt worse than we thought he was at first, and we want Tony. Does she know where he is?"

"No, she doesn't!" exclaimed Jack, before his sister could speak.

"Well, we have a tip about her and another girl being in a hut on Fern Island and being scared by a man," persisted the tall man. "No offense you know, only we thought she could help us out. The man who scared her and her friend may have been Tony."

"I - I didn't see any one - it was dark," explained Cora, before Jack could speak. "Some one approached, fell down and went away again."

"That may have been Tom!" excitedly said the short detective.

"'No, it was -" began Cora.

"Wait a minute," cried Jack. "Before she answers I want to know if you really have a right to the information. How do I know but you may be some one seeking to get evidence for a civil suit for Peters or Tony, and will drag us in as witnesses?"

"Oh, we're not," said the tall man hastily.

"Here's my court-house badge," and he displayed it. "This has nothing to do with a lawsuit. We just want to find Tony. If that wasn't him on the island who scared the girls, who was it? Sure lyshe can't object to telling; it can't hurt her. Who was it?"

Before Cora could answer there was a sound at the door of the hut and a voice exclaimed:

"It was my father!"

There stood Laurel, and the officers shifted their gaze from Cora to her. They started eagerly forward, hoping to get the information they sought from the new witness.

"Tell us about it," urged the short man.

"No, let me, Laurel dear," interrupted Cora. " I can explain

Jack, and have it all over with. Really it's very simple."

Then, without at all going into the details of the mystery of the hermit, which information Cora felt the detectives had no right to possess, she told how she and Laurel had been in the hut and how the unknown man who so frightened, them had turned out to be Laurel's father, and that even now he was under care because of the injury he received.

"And he lived on Fern Island all this while?" asked one of the officers. "Why did he do that?"

"For his health I guess," said Jack sharply. "That doesn't concern your case against Tony, or whatever his name was, and this Peters. You've found out that my sister doesn't know anything to help you in your hunt, and you might as well skip out. This is private ground, you know."

"That doesn't make any difference to the law," growled the short man.

"Oh, yes it does," said Jack sweetly. "You're trespassers as much as any one else if you haven't a warrant, and I don't believe you have."

"No, I guess you're right," admitted the tall man, with as good grace as possible. "Come on," this to his companion, "we can't learn anything here. Let's go see old Ben."

Cora and Laurel had gone into the house. Jack did not want them annoyed again, and he wondered how the men had come to think that Cora might know something of the quarrel between Peters and Tony.

"It was probably just a guess," decided Jack. "There is certainly something like a mystery about the hermit, and -"

He interrupted his thoughts as he saw one of the men coming back.

"Hang it all! I wonder what he wants now?" thought Jack. The man soon informed him.

"I say, do you think the hermit, as you call him, would be well enough to testify in court about this case?" the detective asked.

"What case?" inquired Jack, wondering if the man suspected the reason for the hermit's exile.

"The Peters case."

"No, I don't think he would," was the young man's answer, and once more the man went to his boat.

As he and his companion started off, Jack saw the Petrel containing Bess, Hazel, Walter and Ed swinging up to the small dock. The young, folks looked closely at the two detectives.

"He may have to testify whether he wants to or not!" called the short officer back to Jack who was still watching them. "The law gets what it wants you know. This isn't the only case against Tony. He is an old offender."

"All right, have your own way about it," responded Jack easily, and he noted that the occupants of the Petrel seemed rather alarmed. Then they hastened to disembark as the police boat chugged away, and Jack ran down to meet them.

CHAPTER XXV

AWAKENED MEMORIES

"Oh, where is Cora!" gasped Bess, as she landed at the island rock, and almost fell fainting into Jack's arms.

"Why, she is with Laurel - in the hut. What ever is the matter, Bess?"

"We thought - thought they had taken you all to jail! Oh, those horrible men! Those detectives!"

"You silly," exclaimed Jack, seeing that the poor girl was really exhausted from fright. "Don't you know better than that?"

"But they would not believe us! They made us tell them where you were, and Belle is sick in bed. Their boat passed ours as we were coming in. We had a delay. Oh, we've been so alarmed!"

"Poor Belle," Jack murmured. "Now, Bess, just step up here and make sure for yourself that Cora is just as intact as when you last saw her. I am here to speak for myself. If anything she is better for a night's rest in the open. We expect to start a camp on this plan. It can't be beat."

Ed motioned Jack aside. "Wasn't that the police boat?" he asked.

"Yes, and Cora and I gave them all the clues they wanted.

None at all in other words. They're after Tony."

"Oh! and Cora, is she all right?" Ed questioned further.

"Splendid. Did you hear the latest?"

"Which?" asked Ed, significantly.

"Laurel's father is almost better. The hermit, you know."

"You don't say! Can he testify?" asked Ed.

"He may be able to if they require it. But the queer part is it seems to have been the shock that awakened his brain. I have read of such cases."

Ed was silent, for the girls were returning. Hazel had her brown arms around Cora while Bess looked at Laurel as if she expected every moment her chum might evaporate. Walter towed on behind the little party.

"I must go down to the landing, Jack," Cora said. "I expect a registered letter, and it is most important that I get it at once."

Now this was the very thing that Jack did not want her to do - to get into the crowd of curious ones that would be sure to be congregated about the landing.

"Could I not fetch it? You don't want to leave the girls when they have just come up," Jack interposed.

"I am afraid this time I will have to get my own mail," said Cora with a smile. "Ed can run me down and we will come straight back."

This was finally agreed upon, although Jack did not like the arrangements. He called Ed aside and warned him not to let Cora leave the boat, not to let her speak to anyone, and not to let any one intercept her. "You can tell about those lawyer fellows," he finished. "They might think it their legal duty to interview her, for they know she has been let into the hermit's secret."

Ed readily promised all Jack said, punctuating his remarks with a display of arm muscle which meant that anyone would have to pass pretty close to it to reach Cora while she was in his company. Then they left.

Jack sat down on the ledge near the water. He was not given to the "glooms" but surely he had had more than his share of serious business lately. How it would end was his cause for anxiety. So he was pondering when Laurel touched his arm.

"Father would like to speak to you," she said in a faint voice. "He seems to think he knows you."

Jack jumped up suddenly. "He spoke to me very rationally last night," he said; "perhaps that is what he means."

He followed Laurel into the hut. The old man had gotten up and was as nicely washed and fixed as a sick person is usually when loving hands hover around.

"Good morning, sir," Jack said pleasantly, taking the seat beneath the opening in the boughs that served as a window.

"Good morning, good morning, and a really good morning it is," said the older man. "I wanted to speak with you. Laurel dear, is there not water to fetch?"

Laurel took the cue and hurried out, leaving Jack alone with the hermit.

"Young man," he began, "something has happened to clear my brain. A shock some fifteen years ago, if I have not lost all track of time, almost, if not altogether, deprived me of my reason." He paused and put his hand to his brown forehead, in a motion that seemed more a matter of habit than of necessity.

"Then I came here, or he brought me here. I was all alone. Little Laurel must have been a baby, when one morning I found her at my side. Dear, sweet little cherub. He told me since that her mother had died!"

Jack did not venture an interruption. It all seemed too sacred for the lips of strangers to break in upon.

"Then we lived here. That man - !" He clenched his fist and Jack feared the excitement might be bad for his weakened head.

"Don't let us talk of him," Jack advised. "Let us consider what is best to do now."

"My brave boy!" and the hermit put his arm on Jack's shoulder. "That is always the mighty question for right; what is best to do now?"

A flush had stolen into his sunken cheeks, but Jack could see that it was not years, but trouble, that had marred his handsome face.

"He said I would be convicted - of that... crime!" The words seemed to burn his throat, for he put, his hand up as if to, choke further utterance.

"A crime you never committed," Jack ventured, without having the slightest knowledge of what it might mean to his listener.

"Can you prove it? Can you prove it!" gasped the man and for the moment Jack was frightened. He felt he was again in the presence of the mad hermit of Fern Island.

"Of course we can prove it. My sister has gone now for the absolute proof!" Jack was daring more and more each second. "But you spoke of Breslin. You said you knew him."

"I do! Where is he! Breslin always believed in me, and he could save me now," replied the man.

"Well, listen and try to be calm, or Laurel will not let me talk further to you," Jack cautioned. "Last night you mentioned the name of a wealthy banker, for whom my best friend works. This friend is a mechanical genius and he runs a racer boat for Brendon Breslin, the banker!"

"Where? Here? On these shores?" and the man was panting.

"Only a short distance off. But I tell you, Mr. - ?"

"Starr," volunteered the man.

"Mr. Starr, if you will only get strong enough you can do a, great deal for yourself and Laurel. The night that you fell a man was on this Island. Did you know Jim Peters?"

"Jim Peters!" repeated the hermit. "Yes, he was here the night Laurel went away with that nice young lady who looks like you."

Jack started at that. The night Laurel went away was the night Jim Peters had quarreled with Tony and been hurt.

"Did he come to the hunt?" asked Jack.

"No, but the other man did. Brentano and he quarreled, and he drove Jim Peters down to his boat. I saw them for I was wandering about wishing for Laurel, and I remember it all."

"If that man, Brentano, you call him, chased Peters into the boat did he get in with him?" Jack asked anxiously.

"Yes, I saw them shove off, but Peters was ugly and wanted to come back."

"Did he?"

"I had to hide then, as they might have injured me if they caught me. I did not see the boat go out or come back. I went to one of my many hiding places," finished the old man with evident effort.

"Well, Mr. Starr, you have relieved my mind greatly, and I hope I have not taxed your brain too strongly. But the fact is the detectives are trying to find out about those men and every bit of information helps. The police, you know, like to clear things up to suit themselves," Jack said.

At the word "police," the man winced. Jack noticed the change of manner, and at once turned the subject to that of the health of his listener. He urged him to get up enough strength to leave the island, for Laurel's sake, as well as for his own.

"But I have lived here like a wild man," argued Mr. Starr, "in fact I fear I have grown to be one in ways and manners. Solitude may be good for some, but for those in distress - "

"Exactly. But you are not going to have any more solitude. You see we have invaded your camp, and when my sister Cora makes a discovery she always insists upon developing it. I never did see the beat of Cora for finding things out," and the pride in Jack's voice matched the toss of his handsome head.

"And my little girl will have a friend," mused the elder man. "Well, in moments when I could think, that torturing thought of my dragging her down with me was too much. It drove me back always to the old, old despair." The look of terror, that Jack noticed before came back into the haggard face. It was as if he feared to hope.

Laurel was at the door. Her face was a picture of happiness as she stood there gazing at her father. Her skin was as dark as the leaves that outlined the entrance to the hut; her eyes lighted up the rude archway: and her lithe figure completed the bronze statuette.

Jack's eyes fell upon her in unstinted admiration. Generations of culture are not easily undone even by the wild life of a forest.

"You are better every minute, father," she said simply, "I think the cure you need comes from pleasant company."

"None could be more pleasant than your own, my dear," he answered, "but now I want to go and see my birds. And I must feed that cripple rabbit. He was shot," to Jack, "but the leg is mending nicely. I missed him so, for he knew us so well and would eat from our hands. You see we established a little kingdom here. Laurel was queen and we, the birds and other life creatures, were all her subjects."

Laurel blushed through her tan. "Yes, he had to do something," she said, "else the days would have been too long."

The chug of a motor-boat interrupted them. "That's Cora," said Jack, and so it was.

CHAPTER XXVI

IN SEARCH OF HONOR

Cora brought back with her the letter promised by Brentano in his note of mystery. This time she confided in Laurel her scheme for unraveling the tangled skein in the web of dishonor that had been woven about the strange girl's father.

Ben had spoken to Cora at the Landing. He seemed to think that Cora might know more about the trouble between Peters and Tony than he had expected at first.

"But I don't, Ben," she insisted, while Ed was absent getting mail. "You give me credit for being better able to solve mysteries than I am. Is he worse hurt than they thought, Ben?"

"Much worse, miss. Of course, he's not dangerous, but the officers want Tony the worst way. Now if you could tell where to find him -"

"But I can't," she explained. "They came to me -"

And then she stopped suddenly. If Ben did not know of the visit of the detectives she was not going to tell him. She had had a faint suspicion that Ben might have sent them to her. But he evidently had not.

"Yes - yes," he said eagerly. "You were sayin', Miss Cora, that -"

"Oh, nothing, Ben," she answered quickly. "I think I am really so happy at having helped Laurel, that I don't know what I am saying."

"Yes, indeed you can well be, Miss," and Ben looked at her with what Cora thought a strange gaze. Still, she might be mistaken. Then she made some excuse to stroll away.

Walter had rambled off with Hazel and Bess. The day was now one of those so wonderful in August, when nature seems tired of her anxieties, and rests in a perfect ocean of content. The haze had cleared from the water, the hills were shimmering in the rival honors of sunlight and shadows, and Cedar Lake from far and near was glorious. Not a breeze broke the spell:

"No brisk fairy feet, bend the air, strangely sweet, For nature is wedding her lover!"

This line prompted Cora. Somehow the joy of relief was the one thing that had ever overcome her, and now, although nothing in all, the strange things that had happened around her, or had warped the life of Laurel and her father seemed really cleared away, still there was that odd look on old Ben's face, there was a new light in Laurel's eyes, and something like vigor in the voice of Mr. Starr. Oh, if he could and would only tell about that note! Then everything else might await time for adjustment.

Cora took Jack and Laurel down under the broken chestnut tree to tell them about the letter. It was best, she concluded not to mention it yet to Mr. Starr.

"You know," she began, "that Brentano, that is the man of many names," she explained to Jack, "promised to send me information that would clear Mr. Starr of his supposed crime."

Laurel drew a deep breath. The word crime made her almost shudder.

"And this is to-day's letter." She opened the bulky envelope. "He says so much about a girl's power of influence," Cora explained, as if not wanting to read that part of the letter. Then he says this:

"'I have some excuse for my folly. When I was a very little child my mother died. My farther was an expert mathematician employed by the Mexican government. From a tiny lad I watched him make those fascinating rows of figures, and I always wanted to know what they meant. He told me money, riches, gold, and I got to believe that the way to acquire money was to make figures, and do wonderful things with pen and ink. When I was twelve years old my father died, and I was left, with considerable money, in the care of an old nurse who idolized me. Poor old Maximina! She meant no wrong, but who was to guide me? Then the money was gone and the nurse was also gone. I had to follow some occupation, and a friend coming to America brought me with him. At fifteen I was a bank runner. It was there I met Mr. Starr, the respected first clerk of the bank. He liked me, talked to me and was my friend. Then I got in with a set of so called scientific cranks. I knew something about the ways of hypnotism, and when I wanted money the temptation came."

Cora stopped, for Laurel had clutched at Jack's arm. Her face was a faded yellow and her eyes were twitching.

"Shall we wait for the rest, Laurel?" Cora asked. "Perhaps it is - too painful for you now!"

"Oh, no! It is not pain, it is agony. This boy whom my father befriended!"

"But you see he was not born a scoundrel," Jack interrupted. "He is now trying to make amends."

"Yes," sighed Laurel, "please go on, Cora."

Cora read: "I have kept proofs of everything, but if the

authorities refuse to accept these proofs I am willing to come back to America and give myself up. You will find the papers marked 'bank records' in a chest in the back kitchen of Peters shack. They are sealed in a big tin can marked 'red paint.' What are they saying about Peters? That must be a hard nut for the Lake people to crack, but since they know so much, or they think they know, it might be a good thing to let them find out how little they really do know. I am sorry for poor Peters. He got ugly, however, and it was his own fault?"

As Cora read these last few words her, eyes left the paper. What did he mean? Why did he not say more? He knew Peters' shack held the needed proofs of that forgery case. It would take many days to write to and hear from Mexico. All this was dashing before Cora's confused mind.

"The thing to do," spoke Jack, "is to go to the shack at once. When we find those papers we may believe the man."

"I believe him now," said Laurel, "for all that he says of my father I have heard in his ravings. Poor, dear father! And to think I was too young to help him!"

"It was evidently not a question of age," said Jack, "when one is hypnotized into the belief that he has committed a crime it would take scientific treatment to restore him to his correct view of the case. To remove you from the possibility of this, I suppose, is the very reason that Brentano brought you here."

"We cannot go for the papers to-day," Cora said, "for we must, if possible, get Mr. Starr either to the boys' bungalow, or to our camp. Which do you think, Jack?"

"We will take him to our bungalow, certainly. And it seems to me he is smart and bright enough for the trip now. If we wait later he might have some reaction," Jack replied.

Laurel agreed with him, and presently they broached the matter to Mr. Starr.

"But I cannot go just now," the hermit argued. "I have that little lame rabbit -"

"Why, father," and Laurel folded her arms around him, "don't you think it would be dreadful to disappoint our friends when they have waited the whole night? And they must want to get back to their comfortable quarters."

"Looking at it that way," he faltered, "I suppose I ought to. But how can a man leave the woods when he has been in them for ten years?"

"It must be hard," Cora agreed, "and if you want to come back we could arrange to build you a real camp out here, one in which Laurel might have some comforts. But first you must get strong. Just think of beef tea-broth - can't you smell it?"

"Girl! Girl!" he exclaimed with a real smile brightening his benevolent face, "you have a way! Laurel, we have no trunks to pack," he said, half grimly, "have we?"

"But we have things to take with us," 'and she jumped up so pleased, believing that he had almost, if not entirely, consented to go.

"Where's that rabbit?" asked Jack.

Walter and the girls were coming the other way.

"It's in a mossy bed just back of where Bess stands," said Laurel.

"Then he's the first thing to be packed," said Jack, walking straight for the path where the others stood.

From that time until the Petrel landed at the lower end of Cedar Lake Mr. Starr, the hermit, felt that he was in a dream. At the same time he allowed himself to be guided and managed with the simplicity of a child, for his awakened memory seemed stunned by this new turn of affairs. He was weak, of course, but with all the hands that now crowded around him his every need was well looked after.

"I'll get Dr. Rand," Ed volunteered. "They say he is wonderful on mental cases."

"But he needs rest first," insisted the busy Cora, for she and Laurel had gone directly to the boys' bungalow with Mr. Starr.

Between them all the illness seemed overwhelmed. In fact, the man's eyes, the safest signal of the brain, were as dear as those of the young persons who so eagerly watched his every move.

Dr. Rand came at once. He diagnosed the case as one of mental shock, and called the patient convalescent. A nurse however was called in to hurry the recovery, and this necessitated the renting of another bungalow for the boys.

There had never been more excitement around the wood camp. The boys ran this way and that, each anxious to outdo the other in the accomplishment of something important. Finally Cora suggested that they all go away to make sure that Mr. Starr would have real quiet.

"Can't we go for the papers? To the shack?" Laurel ventured.

"We might," Jack replied. "I see no reason why we should not."

"Let us three go," proposed Cora, "I mean you and Laurel and I, Jack. It might be best not to attract attention."

Once more the Petrel sailed up the lake, this time toward the Everglades. Cora thought of that day when she and Bess dared take the same journey, when the strange man sat at the willowed shore ostensibly making sketches. She thought now that his work then must have been the forging of a letter to hand the poor demented hermit of Fern Island.

"The shack is just over there, Jack," she said, pointing out the willows.

"There's another boat anchored there," Jack said. "It looks like an important craft too."

He had seen it before. It was the very boat in which the detective and the police officer sailed up to the far island the morning they came searching for evidence in the Jones' case.

"The path is narrow," Cora said, "but I happen to know it." She led the way.

"There are men!" exclaimed Laurel as they neared the shack.

Two men were trying to force open the low window. Cora drew back, for one of the men was in uniform.

"I suppose they have not finished the case," Jack ventured, and at that very moment he would have given a great deal to have had his sister and Laurel back at camp.

The men had not yet seen them. They forced open the window, and were now inside.

"Let us turn back," Jack suggested. "They may ask us questions -"

"But the papers," begged Laurel. "They mean so much to father. And what if those men should take them?"

"They will likely take everything they can lay their hands on," Jack answered, "and I suppose it will be best for us to go on."

"Certainly," Cora said, knowing well that it was on her account that Jack hesitated. "They cannot do more than ask questions."

But scarcely had she uttered the words than they saw the two men walk out of the shack, and one of them had the can marked "red paint!"

CHAPTER XXVII

A BOLD RESOLVE

Seeing their precious papers, or the receptacle that was said to contain them, in the hands of the detective, Cora and Laurel both drew back. They could not now demand them, was the thought that flashed to the mind of each, and yet to leave them in possession of the officers, was the very worst thing that could have happened, for there was always the danger of the old story coming up and then the risk to Mr. Starr, after all his years of evading the law!

"They have no right to them," Jack said under his breath.

"Hush!" Cora whispered, "they are going the other way!"

The two men were talking. Suddenly one of them said loudly enough for the listeners to hear:

"It might be dynamite. Not for me! Here goes!" and he carefully set the can down under a bush.

"Yes," said the other man. "You are right. Those two fellows were up to most anything. We will get Mulligan. He could smell dynamite," and with that they turned, took a new path toward the shore, and were soon sailing off in their boat.

For a few moments neither of the three, who were standing there watching, spoke. Then Cora's face brightened.

"They are ours, Laurel's," she said, "and we have a right to take them."

"But the law is queer on such points," Jack argued. "I have known men to be put in jail for what they call interfering with an officer when the officer could not do just what he wanted to with some spunky citizen. I should not like to touch the can of red paint."

"But my father," said Laurel, in the most pleading of tones. "Think what it means! How we have suffered; and now, when this is at our very hands!"

"But suppose it were something other than the papers," cautioned Jack. "Those men had a pretty bad reputation."

"I will take all the risks," declared Cora, and before Jack could detain her she ran to the bush, pushed it aside, and grasped the can.

Jack hurried to take it from her. "Let me have it, Cora; if there is a risk it must be mine."

"All right, Jack dear," she replied, "I am sure there is nothing in it heavier than papers. Wouldn't you think those men could have guessed that?"

"Perhaps they did not want to," said Jack. "You can never tell what they want or mean. They have a system even the country fellows, and it covers a multitude of failures." He shook the can, put it to his ear, rolled it a few feet, picked it up again and laughed. "Mr. Mulligan won't find this can," he said, "Somehow it is attractive, and I am anxious as you girls to see what is in it. If we get in trouble for taking it - well, we'll see," and he led the way down to the Petrel.

On the water they passed the police boat, but the can of "red paint," was snugly resting under Laurel's skirts in the bottom of the boat.

Margaret Penrose

"Will you tell your father at once, Laurel?" Cora asked.

"If he is well enough. Oh, I can scarcely wait. Coral, what wonderful good luck you brought to us," and she reached out her hand to press Cora's.

"Don't be too sure," cautioned the other, "it is not all cleared up yet."

"But I feel sure," she insisted. "Brentano was too clever to do anything half way."

"He certainly was a star," Jack admitted. "But I hope he will not insist upon keeping up the correspondence with Cora. He might give us the hoo-doo."

They were soon at their dock. The Peter Pan was tied, there, and that meant that Paul Hastings was at the bungalow. Jack thought instantly of Paul's employer, the banker, whose name Mr. Starr had mentioned. It did seem now that things were shaping themselves to tell all the story.

"Who is the stranger?" Cora asked, noticing a man in a dressing robe sitting on the little rustic porch.

"I - wonder -" Jack said.

"It's father," almost screamed Laurel, "and he has had his hair cut and his beard taken off! Doesn't he look lovely!"

"It can't be," Cora said hesitatingly. "That man is so young!"

"He's my dear father, just the same," declared the delighted girl, hurrying from the boat up to the bungalow.

The man did not turn his head to greet her, but she was not to be deceived by his little ruse. "What a surprise!" she exclaimed. "I scarcely knew you."

"But you did know me," he replied, with a happy smile. "I feel years and years younger, my dear."

"Indeed you look it," Cora said. "I wonder how you ever hid such good looks."

The nurse was fetching the beef tea, Paul took the cup from her hand. Jack made a wry face at Laurel, indicating that they would have to watch Paul and the pretty new nurse. Then he took the chair nearest Mr. Starr. The can of "red paint" had been safely hidden in a locker of the Petrel.

"Your friend has been telling me the wonders of his fast boat," began Mr. Starr to Jack, speaking of Paul.

"Yes. This is the young man who is employed by Brendon Breslin," Jack replied.

"Employed by Brendon Breslin!" exclaimed Mr. Starr. "Is Mr. Breslin around here?"

"Gone to the city to-day," replied Paul, "but I take him home every night in the Peter Pan. That's what he wants the best boat on the lake for."

"He always believed me, and never wanted me to go away," Mr. Starr said. "And now if I could see him -"

"I don't see why you cannot," put in Jack. "He often rides by here, doesn't he Paul?"

"He thinks this the prettiest end of the lake," Paul replied. "But if you ever knew him and he was your friend I am sure he would be only too glad to make a special trip to see you, for he boasts he never forgets an old friend," Paul said.

"That's him - that's Brendon," exclaimed Mr. Starr, moving uneasily in his chair. "I feel I must be dreaming."

There was a general pause - for realization. Everyone felt indeed it was like a dream, and almost beyond human power to grasp. Mr. Starr swept his hand over his forehead.

"Laurel," he called, "I wonder if I couldn't take a ride in the Peter Pan. Ask the nurse, please - ?"

"Oh, no," objected that young lady. "It would not be wise for you to take another boat ride to-day. We will ask the doctor about it tomorrow."

"Don't be impatient, father," pleaded Laurel. "You must not forget how weak your head has been."

"All right, child. But I want it cleared up," he murmured. "I feel there is no safety for me until I'm vindicated."

"Come on, Jack," whispered Cora. "We must open that can."

Paul was leaving. Cora and Jack walked to the dock with him. He assured them both that Mr. Breslin would call very soon, and also promised to be on hand on the following Wednesday evening when the girls and boys were planning to have a celebration.

"They will never know but that it is really paint," Cora remarked, as she and Jack walked boldly up the path with the precious tin can. "Just take it around to the back, and be careful opening it."

"Dynamite?" asked Jack with a smile.

"No, but you might damage something," she replied.

"No worry about damaging myself?" he persisted. "Well, Cora, I hope it contains - some jewels. Wouldn't that be nice?"

There was no chance for further conversation. Cora went to the porch while her brother carried out her instructions.

Presently she made some excuse, and left Laurel alone, talking with her father.

She found Jack sitting on the wash bench with the can opened and in his hands.

"Didn't go off?" she asked, peering into the tin.

"Not a go," replied Jack, "but look! What did I tell you! There's an envelope marked for Laurel, and feel! Are they not stones? Diamonds or pearls?"

"You romancer!" exclaimed Cora, as she felt the bulky envelope. "I admit they do feel like stones, but they may be merely corals. But oh, Jack! Do let me see!"

"Lets call Laurel," he suggested. "We cannot read any of those papers. They are for her, or her father, to open."

"Oh, of course," and Cora looked rebuked. "I had no idea of reading anything, but I thought we should make sure of what was in the can before we got Laurel excited over it," and she slipped around the side of the bungalow to beckon to Laurel.

The girl's face turned white when she saw why she was wanted. "I am so afraid of disappointment," she murmured with a sigh.

"Well, there's something in here," Jack told her. "Look at this," and he handed her the heavy envelope.

She read her name - then she tore open the paper. A necklace fell out on her lap!

"Mother's!" she exclaimed, pressing the golden chain to her lips reverently. "Darling mother's!"

"And the stones are amethysts!" Cora exclaimed as Laurel held up the gems.

"Yes, it was father's wedding present to mother," Laurel told them. "Oh, I scarcely know how to tell him all this."

"Tony was a pretty decent robber after all," remarked Jack. "He kept them for you, at any rate."

"Yes, poor man. Perhaps, as he said, his one temptation was to do clever things with a pen. Let us look over the papers."

"Perhaps your father had best see you do that," Jack suggested.

"Oh no. I think I had better know first," Laurel insisted. "Let me open this," and she carefully broke a large red seal on a packet of documents yellow with age.

Paper after paper she took out. Finally what she was looking for she found. It was a check that had been cashed and cancelled! It bore the marks also of "forgery!"

"That's it," she exclaimed. "That is the ten thousand dollar check!"

CHAPTER XXVIII

ALL ENDS WELL-CONCLUSION

"I remember it all - it's like a book open before me!"

Laurel had insisted upon her father reclining in the hammock, and she was now fussing with his pillows, that he might nestle deeper in their softness. It was he who was speaking. On the porch sat Brendon Breslin, looking into Peter Starr's face like one enchanted. There was Cora moving a big fan so that apparently without her doing it, the breeze reached the man in the hammock. Jack was there and Ed was inside the bungalow teasing Walter who had "discovered" the new nurse. Hazel, Bess and Belle were busy - there was to be "something doing."

A day had passed since the opening of the can of "red paint." In fact it was the evening following that eventful performance. Paul had only to say "Peter Starr'" to Mr. Breslin, and the latter was ready to be at the bungaloafers' camp. So the story was unwinding.

"Do you really feel able to talk?" asked the millionaire banker. "I will insist now - you got, the better of me once, Peter."

"Yes, Mr. Starr," Cora added to the request. "Do be careful."

"And she asks me to be careful!" He actually seized Cora in his trembling arms. "She! Why she risked her life for us. It was she who found my Laurel! She who came to us at night to be sure we would not repel her! She who followed up that -"

"Oh, please, hush!" Cora begged, "or it will be she who causes your relapse," she insisted.

"Indeed no," and the man held in his hands before him the flushed face of Cora. "What you have done cannot be told of in this rude way."

"Father, I'll be jealous," said Laurel, trying to relieve the tension.

Cora slipped away. It was Mr. Breslin who spoke next.

"And you really remember?" he asked of Mr. Starr. "How was it that you ran away?"

"The bank president's name had been forged to a check for ten thousand dollars!"

"Yes, I know that well," said Mr. Breslin.

"And they traced the forgery to me!"

"But you knew you were innocent!"

"I knew it, but I was frightened by the accusation, and they had found trials of the signature in my desk!"

"I have a letter that explains that," Cora imparted, and then she told how Brentano had confessed to the forgery, and to his almost hypnotic influence over Mr. Starr.

"And then?" inquired Mr. Breslin.

"Brentano told me I must go. He fixed everything. I have been on the island ten years," and the hermit sighed heavily.

"How did you live?" asked the banker.

"He fixed that," and there was bitterness in his tone. "He brought me letters regularly. These were alleged to come from those who would prosecute me if I did not keep on paying money!"

At this statement the banker dashed up from his seat. "The scoundrel!" he almost hissed. "He ought to be jailed! If I had him here I'd do it too. I'm mayor of this borough."

"Oh, Mr. Breslin!" exclaimed Laurel. "He must not have been entirely bad. See how he saved the papers - the proofs - and how he kept for me my mother's jewels."

"That's the sentimental mire that foreign criminals wallow in," he replied with irony. "I cannot see that it mitigates the crime."

"And yet," interrupted Mr. Starr, "see how the influence of a mere girl turned him to right? I did like that boy!"

Cora and Laurel had crept away to the far end of the porch. Two men came up the path.

"Hello!" said Mr. Breslin. "Officers!"

There was surprise on the officers' faces when they saw Mr. Breslin, their superior officer, the mayor of Cedar Lake, sitting on the porch. Greetings were exchanged and finally they ventured to make known their mission.

They had heard that someone saw Cora Kimball take the state's evidence - the can of "red paint!"

"But what was a can of paint?" asked the mayor. "As if a girl would want that," and   his voice was almost mocking.

"Well, it might have been dynamite," and the man who wore brass buttons shook his head sagely.

"A girl steal a can of dynamite," repeated Mr. Breslin mockingly.

The officers were trying to see who was in the hammock. But the man therein sank back into the cushions, while Jack carelessly slipped his chair directly in front of him.

"Why didn't you take it when you saw it?" asked the town's mayor.

"Well," explained the other man, "we didn't fancy the blow-up. We went for Mulligan who knows about such things, and when we came back it was gone."

"You had better tell that story before the jury," and the sarcasm in Mr. Breslin's tone was unmistakable. "Suppose you tell them that a girl took what you were afraid to touch!"

Seeing that it was useless to argue with the mayor, they turned to leave.

"Wait," he said good naturedly, "I have my boat here. Take a ride with me. It's better than walking the dusty roads. Good evening," he said. "Mr. Fennelly," (to Mr. Starr,) "I hope you will regain your health by the time your son has to return to college!"

"Fennelly," said one officer to the other. "That's not the name, it was Starr! We're on the wrong trail." And they hurried away. Thus had Mr. Breslin saved the hermit from having to testify.

"Laurel," Cora said wearily, "let us go for a little walk. My nerves are all snarled up, and only a walk will unravel them. We will have time to go as far as the hemlocks before those girls and boys make up their minds to disband."

"But it is dark," objected Laurel.

"All the better; the quiet will be more effective. Come on,

Laurel. Surely you do not mind a dark evening."

"Oh, no indeed, Cora," she replied, winding her arm, about her friend's waist, "but I was thinking it might shower."

"Oh, we could beat any shower," insisted, Laurel, "Come let us get away before they miss us."

It was getting very dark indeed, but they heeded it not, so interested were they in their chat.

They talked of many things, as girls will, and Laurel told much of her half-wild life, on Fern Island, while Cora related some of her own experiences. Then they returned to the house, where they found the others assembled.

"Let's have some fun," suggested Walter.

"I vote for charades," said Jack. "I'll be a fish."

"All right!" exclaimed the nurse, entering into the spirit of the fun, "here's where you swim!" and she poured a glass of water down Jack's back. He accepted the challenge and made exaggerated motions as if he were struggling in deep water. There was a gale of laughter, and that was the beginning of a gay time. The troubles of the past seemed all forgotten.

The now happy party remained together for several days and in the meanwhile there were many developments.

Through the efforts of Mr. Breslin everything regarding the former hermit was cleared up, and his name was once more restored to its untarnished honor. There was absolutely no charge against him, and on learning this, his health took a big change for the better. As for Laurel, she was happier than she had been in many years.

The injury to Jim Peters did not amount to as much as had been feared at first and he gradually recovered. There was no trace of "Tony," as everyone called Brentano. The search for him was given up, but the officers who had been fooled by the can of "red paint" had a hard time living down the joke against them. Cora destroyed all the correspondence she had received. It was like a bad dream, all but that part about helping Laurel and her father, and she wanted to forget it. Laurel also destroyed the letter Jack had picked up the night of the search. It was one from Brentano, and she, too, wanted no remembrance of him. This epistle had a slight connection with the mystery.

Old Ben proved a good friend and Cora was sorry for the momentary feeling she had had against him. He showed the boys many woodland haunts and took them to secret fishin' "holes" unknown to the general public. The lads voted him a "brick."

It was a bright, beautiful day and every one was happy - happy because of the fine weather and because everything had turned out so well.

"I feel just like doing something!" exclaimed Cora, who, came in from a walk in the woods.

"What, sis?" asked Jack, making a grab for her which she adroitly avoided.

"Oh - almost anything. Since so much of our summer was spoiled in exploring and in solving mysteries, suppose we dispel the gloom with a spell of reckless gaiety."

"Suppose," agreed Hazel. "What shall it be? I vote for water fun. We can have parties and that sort of stuff all winter."

"Fishing! The very thing!" exclaimed Cora, "and give prizes for fish, near fish, and no fish."

"Oh, the boys would be sure to win on the fish number," said Hazel, "but let's try it. We have to have live bait, I suppose."

"And we can haul the bait nets. Did you ever see them cast one of those thirty feet ones?" asked Cora.

"Never," replied Hazel. "But when shall we start, and what do we start? I'll dig for worms."

"To-night we will go for the bait, and you can go out with a lantern in the darkest parts of the woods to dig for worms," Cora said, knowing, that this would put an end to Hazel's offer.

"In the woods? In our own back yard. I know how to turn stones over. I have often helped Paul," Hazel attested.

But it was casting the big thirty foot net that really furnished the best sport. It was dropped from a rowboat by Bess and Cora while Laurel and Belle rowed. Then when it was all spread out they had to row very quickly in a circle to close the bottom and to drag in the unsuspecting little fishes that were to make the live bait.

The first trial resulted in Belle resigning as oarsman. She had lost a gold-rimmed side-comb overboard, besides getting very wet when the boat turned suddenly and "took a wave."

"I can row alone," insisted Laurel. "Cora and Hazel must manage the net."

This time they did bring up some fish - a whole drove of wiggling, frightened little minnies.

"How do we get them out?" asked Bess, more frightened than the fish.

"Pick them out and put them in the bait box," Cora explained, while Bess made a negative face.

"It seems a shame to use them for bait," Laurel said, as on the pier they opened the net carefully and saw the pretty silvery things slip around. "Couldn't we put them some place to grow up?"

"The fish-orphans' home," suggested Cora. "But I must have a few. You know, girls, fish have no brains. That's the reason I suppose they go into the brain business when they get a chance at humans."

The very next afternoon the girl's fishing party rowed out from Center Landing. Walter went along to take the fish off the hooks of Belle and Bess who declared they would never be able to do that. The other boy's composed a rival party.

Ben was at the landing, and he wished them all sorts of luck besides telling them the secret spots where fish dwelt. They went deep into the cove, as Ben said the pickerel loved to lay in the grasses there.

Bess and Belle insisted upon following the directions on the box of a patent "plug" they had purchased and cast near a lily pond, reeling in so slowly that Hazel and Cora had both had "strikes" before the twins saw their white make believe fish come to the surface. This sort of casting was for bass of course.

"I've got one! I've got one!" shouted Cora, as she pulled in a handsome big, black bass.

This won the first and last prize, for it was an exceptionally fine specimen.

"We knew you would have the best luck, Cora," Hazel said without malice, as she dragged up a very small, scared sunny. "We knew it. You always do."

"It isn't luck," added Laurel, "It's skill. She knew that she must pull up as soon as the fish struck. I lost something. It might have been a snake but it got away because I was not quick enough."

There was quite a laugh when Jack, after a hard struggle, during which he protested that he must have the biggest pickerel in the lake, pulled in a large mud turtle. Later, however, he redeemed himself by catching one of the long fish which gave him quite a battle of the line. The other boys did well, and the girls were not far behind them.

"Well," remarked Cora, during a lull in the proceedings when they had gone ashore to eat the lunch they had brought along, "we really haven't had so much fun as this since we came to the lake. There was so much excitement."

"There are other vacations coming," predicted Ed. "There is no telling what may happen since she has learned to adjust a spark plug, and regulate a timer."

Ed was right; there were other adventures in store for the motor girls, and what they consisted of will be related in the next volume of this series to be entitled "The Motor Girls on the Coast or The Waif from the Sea."

The afternoon waned. No one felt like going fishing after lunch. Besides, as Cora said, they, had enough, and they were all cleaned up from the "mess" of baiting hooks.

And now, for a time we will take leave of the girls, as they are sitting on the shady shores of Cedar Lake, talking - talking - and the boys listening, with occasional remarks.

"And I'm so glad it all came out right," Cora murmured. "You are to go to school with me, Laurel - mother has planned about that."

"And it was so good of Mr. Breslin to arrange to have father do clerical work for him," added the woodland maid. "Oh, how lovely everything is!"

And the sun, sinking to rest, cast a rosy glow over the peaceful waters of the lake.

Choose from Thousands of 1stWorldLibrary Classics By

Adolphus WilliamWard
Aesop
Agatha Christie
Alexander Aaronsohns
Alexander Kielland
Alexandre Dumas
Alfred Gatty
Alfred Ollivant
Alice Duer Miller
Alice Turner Curtis
Alice Dunbar
Ambrose Bierce
Amelia E. Barr
Andrew Lang
Andrew McFarland Davis
Anna Sewell
Annie Besant
Annie Hamilton Donnell
Annie Payson Call
Anton Chekhov
Arnold Bennett
Arthur Conan Doyle
Arthur Ransome
Atticus
B. M. Bower
Basil King
Bayard Taylor
Ben Macomber
Booth Tarkington
Bram Stoker
C. Collodi
C. E. Orr
C. M. Ingleby
Carolyn Wells
Catherine Parr Traill
Charles A. Eastman
Charles Dickens
Charles Dudley Warner
Charles Farrar Browne
Charles Ives
Charles Kingsley
Charles Lathrop Pack
Charles Whibley
Charles Willing Beale
Charlotte M. Braeme
Charlotte M.Yonge
Clair W. Hayes
Clarence Day Jr.
Clarence E. Mulford

Clemence Housman
Confucius
Cornelis DeWitt Wilcox
Cyril Burleigh
D. H. Lawrence
Daniel Defoe
David Garnett
Don Carlos Janes
Donald Keyhole
Dorothy Kilner
Dougan Clark
E. Nesbit
E.P.Roe
E. Phillips Oppenheim
Edgar Allan Poe
Edgar Rice Burroughs
Edith Wharton
Edward J. O'Biren
John Cournos
Edwin L. Arnold
Eleanor Atkins
Elizabeth Cleghorn
Gaskell
Elizabeth Von Arnim
Ellem Key
Emily Dickinson
Erasmus W. Jones
Ernie Howard Pie
Ethel Turner
Ethel Watts Mumford
Eugenie Foa
Eugene Wood
Evelyn Everett-Green
Everard Cotes
F. J. Cross
Federick Austin Ogg
Ferdinand Ossendowski
Francis Bacon
Francis Darwin
Frances Hodgson Burnett
Frank Gee Patchin
Frank Harris
Frank Jewett Mather
Frank L. Packard
Frederick Trevor Hill
Frederick Winslow Taylor
Friedrich Kerst
Friedrich Nietzsche
Fyodor Dostoyevsky

Gabrielle E. Jackson
Garrett P. Serviss
Gaston Leroux
George Ade
Geroge Bernard Shaw
George Ebers
George Eliot
George MacDonald
George Orwell
George Tucker
George W. Cable
George Wharton James
Gertrude Atherton
Grace E. King
Grant Allen
Guillermo A. Sherwell
Gulielma Zollinger
Gustav Flaubert
H. A. Cody
H. B. Irving
H. G. Wells
H. H. Munro
H. Irving Hancock
H. Rider Haggard
H. W. C. Davis
Hamilton Wright Mabie
Hans Christian Andersen
Harold Avery
Harold McGrath
Harriet Beecher Stowe
Harry Houidini
Helent Hunt Jackson
Helen Nicolay
Hendy David Thoreau
Henrik Ibsen
Henry Adams
Henry Ford
Henry Frost
Henry James
Henry Jones Ford
Henry Seton Merriman
Henry Wadsworth
Longfellow
Henry W Longfellow
Herbert A. Giles
Herbert N. Casson
Herman Hesse
Homer
Honore De Balzac

Horace Walpole
Horatio Alger, Jr.
Howard Pyle
Howard R. Garis
Hugh Lofting
Hugh Walpole
Humphry Ward
Ian Maclaren
Israel Abrahams
J.G.Austin
J. Henri Fabre
J. M. Barrie
J. Macdonald Oxley
J. S. Knowles
J. Storer Clouston
Jack London
Jacob Abbott
James Allen
James Lane Allen
James Andrews
James Baldwin
James DeMille
James Joyce
James Oliver Curwood
James Oppenheim
James Otis
Jane Austen
Jens Peter Jacobsen
Jerome K. Jerome
John Burroughs
John F. Kennedy
John Gay
John Glasworthy
John Habberton
John Joy Bell
John Milton
John Philip Sousa
Jonathan Swift
Joseph Carey
Joseph Conrad
Joseph Jacobs
Julian Hawthrone
Julies Vernes
Justin Huntly McCarthy
Kakuzo Okakura
Kenneth Grahame
Kate Langley Bosher
L. A. Abbot
L. T. Meade
L. Frank Baum
Laura Lee Hope

Laurence Housman
Leo Tolstoy
Leonid Andreyev
Lewis Carroll
Lilian Bell
Lloyd Osbourne
Louis Tracy
Louisa May Alcott
Lucy Fitch Perkins
Lucy Maud Montgomery
Lydia Miller Middleton
Lyndon Orr
M. H. Adams
Margaret E. Sangster
Margaret Vandercook
Maria Edgeworth
Maria Thompson Daviess
Mariano Azuela
Marion Polk Angellotti
Mark Overton
Mark Twain
Mary Austin
Mary Cole
Mary Rowlandson
Mary Wollstonecraft
Shelley
Max Beerbohm
Myra Kelly
Nathaniel Hawthrone
O. F. Walton
Oscar Wilde
Owen Johnson
P.G.Wodehouse
Paul and Mable Thorn
Paul G. Tomlinson
Paul Severing
Peter B. Kyne
Plato
R. Derby Holmes
R. L. Stevenson
Rabindranath Tagore
Rahul Alvares
Ralph Waldo Emmerson
Rene Descartes
Rex E. Beach
Richard Harding Davis
Richard Jefferies
Robert Barr
Robert Frost
Robert Gordon Anderson
Robert L. Drake

Robert Lansing
Robert Michael Ballantyne
Robert W. Chambers
Rosa Nouchette Carey
Ross Kay
Rudyard Kipling
Samuel B. Allison
Samuel Hopkins Adams
Sarah Bernhardt
Selma Lagerlof
Sherwood Anderson
Sigmund Freud
Standish O'Grady
Stanley Weyman
Stella Benson
Stephen Crane
Stewart Edward White
Stijn Streuvels
Swami Abhedananda
Swami Parmananda
T. S. Ackland
The Princess Der Ling
Thomas A. Janvier
Thomas A Kempis
Thomas Anderton
Thomas Bailey Aldrich
Thomas Bulfinch
Thomas De Quincey
Thomas H. Huxley
Thomas Hardy
Thomas More
Thornton W. Burgess
U. S. Grant
Valentine Williams
Victor Appleton
Virginia Woolf
Walter Scott
Washington Irving
Wilbur Lawton
Wilkie Collins
Willa Cather
Willard F. Baker
William Makepeace Thackeray
William W. Walter
Winston Churchill
Yei Theodora Ozaki
Young E. Allison
Zane Grey

www.ingramcontent.com/pod-product-compliance
Lightning Source LLC
Chambersburg PA
CBHW030316180626
46810CB00003B/1104